SURVIVE THE PANIC

Nuclear Survival: Southern Grit Book Three

HARLEY TATE

SURVIVE THE PANIC

Nuclear Survival: Southern Grit Book Three

With no help in sight, could you make the hard choices?

After risking everything, Grant and Leah Walton are finally reunited. But it's no happy ending. As the reality of the situation dawns on their neighbors, the Waltons find themselves the subject of more than idle curiosity.

Not everyone can be trusted.

People they counted as friends now look at them with suspicion and fear. Faced with neighbors determined to take all they have, Grant and Leah prepare to leave. But strangers have other plans.

If someone threatens all that you hold dear, could you fight back?

In a world without enforcement, rules mean nothing. When a band of thieves turn a neighborhood disagreement into an all-out war, Grant and Leah must find the strength to not only fight, but survive. Not everyone will make it.

The attack is only the beginning.

Survive The Panic is book three in *Nuclear Survival: Southern Grit*, a post-apocalyptic thriller series following ordinary people struggling to survive after a nuclear attack on the Unites States plunges the nation into chaos.

Subscribe to Harley's newsletter and receive *First Strike*, the prequel to the *Nuclear Survival* saga, absolutely free.

www.harleytate.com/subscribe

CHAPTER ONE

GRANT

2078 Rose Valley Lane
Smyrna, Georgia
Sunday, 12:30 p.m.

Black hair sticking up in all directions greeted Grant as he peered through the peephole of his front door. He opened the door and Oliver ducked past him before Grant could say hello.

"I've got something you have to—" Oliver jerked to a stop as he spotted Leah. "Whoa. You look like shit."

With thick glasses, skinny jeans, and a habit of blurting out the obvious, Oliver had never been one of their close friends. The end of the world as Grant knew it changed more than the food and gas supply.

He shut the door and locked it. "Leah, you know Oliver from the neighborhood, right?"

His wife held out a hand with a smile. "I think we met last year at the Labor Day party."

Oliver shifted his messenger bag and shook her hand. "What happened to you?"

She glanced at Grant as she touched the swollen skin beneath her stitches. "Everything from a car accident to a mean cat to a joy ride through a farm."

Grant swallowed. They hadn't even had a chance to talk about what happened the past week. His wife had been through so much. He opened his mouth to say something, but Leah laughed and cut him off. "I'll fill you in later, honey."

Oliver's head swiveled as he looked first at Grant and then Leah. "I feel like I just walked into a sitcom and I missed the punchline."

"It's been a rough few days." Grant motioned to Oliver's bag. "What's so important?"

Oliver fished out his laptop. "You need to see what I've found."

Grant ushered Oliver into the living room and they sat beside each other on the couch.

As he popped open his laptop, Oliver explained. "As soon as I got back from the sporting goods store, I set up the solar panels and charged all the battery packs. I had enough energy to run my laptop for days."

"That can't be why you're here."

"It's not." Oliver's fingers flew across the keyboard and screenshots of chat conversations opened up. "There wasn't a cloud in the sky last night, so I stayed awake and set up my gear in the backyard. I managed to access the dark web via satellite connection around two in the morning."

Grant shifted. The dark web was where the hackers at the convention in Charlotte found out about the attacks. It was the whole reason he was outside the blast radius when the bombs went off. But there was more disinformation out there than facts. "Why not the regular news? There have to be places in the US that have power."

"What about the small newspapers? A television station in Alaska?" Leah eased into the overstuffed chair across from the couch and Faith, the little dog who'd adopted Grant and the now-defunct Cutlass, curled up in her lap.

Grant wished more than anything to take his wife away from the impending chaos and keep her safe. But he knew she would never agree. Not when they had friends and neighbors who might need help.

Oliver interrupted Grant's spiraling thoughts. "I've tried to find news stations, but it's a no-go. Most of the hosting companies are blown to bits. The ones that are still functional are so over capacity, nothing will load. I wasted half an hour giving it a try and my internet connection bogged down to a crawl."

Grant pinched the back of his neck. It was obvious once he gave it some thought. He'd already waved off any hope of a cell connection or major metro internet providers, but he'd forgotten about the servers themselves.

Although on an ordinary day, anyone could fire up a

computer and get on a website authored by someone halfway around the world, the servers that housed most of the web hosting were consolidated into a handful of areas. All of which were large metropolitan centers, most of which had been blown to smithereens.

Oliver scooted forward and pulled up multiple windows on his computer. "The satellite connection is spotty at best and trying to pull up a news outlet when everyone else is doing the same thing was going to wreck any chance I had of finding information. So I pulled up a Tor browser and managed to get in a chat room where a bunch of hackers were discussing it."

Grant thought back to his conversation in Charlotte. Baker and Midge had warned him and it turned out they both told the truth. He couldn't discount what Oliver discovered even if no one could verify the source.

The dark web might be the only source of reliable information now. He leaned closer. "What did you find?"

Oliver pushed his glasses up his nose. "According to a few different sources, a bomb did go off in Washington, DC. The president, most of his cabinet, the senate, house, you name it—all presumed dead."

Leah gasped, and Grant flicked his eyes up to meet hers. Neither said a word, but the question was obvious: if everyone was dead, who was running the country?

Oliver answered their thoughts. "An interim government has been set up at someplace called Fort Monroe."

Grant snorted. "You can't be serious."

"Why? What is that place?"

"I went there once on a high school field trip to DC years ago. It's basically an island off the coast of Virginia. Think the American version of a castle, stone walls, moat all around it. Jefferson Davis was held there after the Union captured him in the Civil War."

Oliver brushed off the history lesson. "Well, whatever it used to be, it's now the White House, Capitol, and everything else related to the federal government."

Grant ran a hand down his face. From what he remembered, the fort managed to stay in Union hands all through the Civil War, even with most of Virginia seceding. Today it sat across from Norfolk Navy Base. He could still remember standing on the beach at Fort Monroe and seeing the aircraft carriers in a line across the river.

It was a better place than many to reconstitute the government of the United States. But would it matter? A bunker without communication with the outside world wouldn't be much good to anyone.

He leaned in to get a look at Oliver's screen. Chats between various anonymous users filled the windows, all talking about the bombs and the government and what would happen next.

"Who's in charge?" Leah spoke up for the first time since Oliver broke the news. Grant could hear the fear in her voice.

"No one knows. I've seen rumors that it's CIA or FBI or some general in the army."

Grant raised an eyebrow. "Not an elected official?"

"I don't know." Oliver pulled up another screen.

"With all the major cities hit, the typical channels to gain information are gone. Everyone is scrambling to backdoor into the handful of smaller municipalities that are still accessible. But with the amount of consolidation that's happened in the last few decades, it's been almost impossible."

He leaned back on the couch. "Local police don't even have their own criminal databases anymore. It's all federal now. Without Washington operational, even the small towns are shut out of their usual sources of information."

Grant pointed at the screen. "So where are all these people you've been talking to? Every hacker I've ever met has lived in a big city."

Oliver cut him a glance. "Then you haven't met the good ones. Guys who spend their days basically underground don't live in the center of Manhattan. Besides, a lot of them are ex-pats. They don't live in the US anymore."

He punched a few keys and pulled up another screen. "But this guy, he claims to live in Anchorage."

Grant leaned closer. A screenshot of a conversation with someone named Moose69 filled the computer screen. "I take it that Moose guy is your source?"

Oliver nodded. "He got into the FBI server in Anchorage and has been poking around. Says it's chaos. Eighty percent of their agents were killed in the attacks. The ones left are mostly junior agents on their first assignments in small towns or older guys pushing paper until retirement."

Grant frowned. "I get that talent would flock to the cities, but didn't they have any warning? Didn't they know? The attacks were all over the dark web hours beforehand. That's why I left Charlotte. That's how I knew to come home."

Oliver glanced at Grant. "If that's true, then someone in the FBI had to know. They have an entire cyber security department. Next time I can connect, I'll see if there's any more information."

Leah cleared her throat. "Is anyone taking responsibility?"

Oliver shook his head. "Not yet."

"Isn't that strange?"

"Very."

Grant's wife tucked her legs up underneath her and Faith shifted to make room. The fluffy little thing looked so different clean and brushed than she did when Grant found her. But despite her show dog looks, Grant knew she was tough.

He focused on her black toe pads and his frown deepened. Nothing about this sat right with him, and the more Oliver talked, the less comfortable Grant became. He shook his head. "Whenever terrorists strike they're quick to come out and take responsibility. Why not now?"

Oliver shrugged. "Maybe it wasn't terrorists."

"What are you saying?" Leah shuddered in the chair and Faith let out a whimper. "We're at war?"

"It's one possibility."

Grant frowned. "Whatever country was responsible

would own it, too. Has anyone seen any uptick in ocean traffic? Are any naval ships deploying for us?"

"Not that I've seen."

"There's more going on here than we think. Nothing you've found adds up."

Oliver began to close his open windows. "At least we know it's not aliens."

Grant snorted. "True." He watched Oliver closed all the screenshots until a single name caught his eye. "Hold it." He leaned in. *MFly.* "I know that name."

He struggled to remember. Was it the girl in Charlotte? The boy who discovered it all first? He couldn't remember their handles. Hell, they probably changed them all the time.

But he couldn't shake the feeling he knew this one. He pointed at the name. "Next time you're online, ping this one. I think I've met MFly before."

Oliver turned to look out the window, but plywood greeted him instead. He frowned. "You're taking this whole 'be prepared' thing a little too seriously, you know?"

Grant laughed. "You can never be too prepared."

CHAPTER TWO

LEAH

2078 Rose Valley Lane
Smyrna, Georgia
Sunday, 2:00 p.m.

Leah couldn't stop the tremor in her hands. Half of what Grant and Oliver spoke about as they hunched over the laptop made no sense, but her husband's knowledge of the web and all its hidden corners vastly exceeded her own.

She smiled at her husband and excused herself from the room. Once upon a time, their house had been a comfortable place to live. Now it smelled like a construction site with boarded-up windows and lanterns for light.

The second floor was the only place it still felt like home.

Faith trotted after her as she climbed the stairs to the

master bedroom. With afternoon light pouring in the bathroom window, Leah stopped in front of the mirror and took stock.

The swelling around her wound improved by the hour. With multiple doses of Fish Mox in her system, the infection was clearing. No fluid oozed from the stitches and she could see the clear threads holding her scalp together.

In a week or two, she would be able to cut the stitches and let the wound heal the rest of the way on its own. She leaned closer, squinting at her reflection. The gash would scar something fierce, but maybe in time, her hair would grow back to cover it.

Leah ran a hand over her prickly scalp. Unfortunately, that would take some time. For months, she'd look either vaguely threatening or like a cancer patient on her deathbed, depending on the day. No one looked at a pale bald woman and thought positive thoughts.

She exhaled and glanced down at the little dog sitting patiently by her feet. "Wherever did you come from?"

Scooping her up into her arms, Leah smiled. Never had she thought they'd have a pet. Grant sneezed when he looked at a cat and Leah never had a dog growing up. They usually made her nervous.

But not Faith. She rubbed the dog under her chin before setting her back on the ground. "We're lucky to have you. All that fur is a welcome distraction from reality."

Walking out of the bathroom, Leah paused at the

sliding glass door. She stared out at the broken and ruined skyline for a moment before sucking in a breath and opening the door. It slid back on the track with a groan and Leah stepped outside.

From their vantage point northwest of downtown, they had always enjoyed one of the best views in Smyrna. Not anymore. Where high-rises and a burgeoning metropolis used to sit, nothing remained apart from a single skyscraper. It sat alone, a bite taken out of its side like Godzilla had wandered through with an empty stomach.

How long before it collapsed? A matter of days, she figured. And then it would be like Atlanta never existed. The business district, the government buildings, all the inner workings of an entire state, gone in seconds.

She wrapped her arms around her middle as she stared. If what Oliver said was true, what future did the United States have? Without a functioning federal government, would the military mobilize? Were there even enough servicemembers left to help the country keep the peace?

Working her lower lip back and forth between her teeth, the reality of it all hit Leah full force. For the past week, she'd been on a mission to find Grant. That's all she had thought about. Every time fears for the future crowded in, she had pushed them away.

How could she think about the future when her husband was out there somewhere? Possibly dead or dying?

It had taken all of her focus to make it to Hampton

and then the last of her resolve to escape and drive home. Now that she was reunited with Grant, she could finally breathe and think and confront the terror head-on.

They had to assume the national government was gone. That meant states, counties, and cities were the only sources of infrastructure left. With the capitol of Georgia being Atlanta, the prospects of their state having a working government were slim to none.

Did the Smyrna city government survive? Would the Cobb County police force still be patrolling? Would officers show up for work without power or working police cruisers?

She sucked in a breath. Preparing for the worst was the best strategy. They had to assume the police and city government were gone and never coming back. That meant the neighborhood was on its own.

Leah thought about her sister's town of Hampton and its blockade. No one in and no one out. Isolation and protectionism.

It wasn't the worst idea now. If the neighborhood banded together and blocked the main entrances, they might be able to hold on to their little patch of the country. The Chattahoochee River flowed around the northwestern corner of the neighborhood. They could stake out the section abutting their community and claim it as their own.

That meant fish and water and enough land to grow a community garden. But it would take work.

Leah's neighbors would need to see the benefit of

banding together. They would need to come to terms with this new reality.

She thought about Dr. Phillips and his neighbors. Fear and disbelief kept them from protecting themselves when faced with a nuclear threat. Surely now that the worst had happened, her neighbors would be willing to try.

"Not the best view anymore, is it?"

Leah jumped at the sound of her husband's voice.

"Didn't mean to scare you."

She smiled. "It's okay. I was lost in thought."

He slipped his arms around her waist and hugged her tight. "I need to go to Oliver's place and see if we can get back online. I'm convinced that hacker he talked to is the girl from the Hack-A-Thon."

"The one who told you about the threat?"

"The one who confirmed it. If I can reach back out to her, we can find out what's happening in other cities. If I remember right, she was headed to Chicago."

Leah twisted in her husband's grasp. "And she's alive? How?"

"That's one of the things I'd like to find out."

"Is she trustworthy?"

Grant hesitated. "She told me the truth about the bombs. At first, she didn't even believe it. Another kid she sat beside found it first. It was only after she started digging that she took it seriously."

"Thank goodness she did."

Her husband nodded. "Otherwise I'd be dead."

"We both would be." Leah eased out of her husband's

embrace and shook out her arms. The stress of the past week stiffened her muscles and lodged in her bones. She nodded toward the door. "Go. If you can reach the hacker, find out all you can."

"It shouldn't take more than a few hours."

Leah walked over to the closet and pulled out a pair of sneakers.

"You don't have to come with me."

"I'm not." She slipped her feet into the shoes and called to the dog. "Faith and I are going on a walk."

"Do you really think that's wise? Shouldn't you rest?"

Leah flashed her husband a smile. "If America is under attack from a bunch of terrorists or at war with some nation that is about to invade, we need to prepare."

"I've already boarded up the house. You'll be safe inside."

Leah stepped forward and placed a hand on Grant's chest. "That's a good start. But we need friends, too."

Grant shook his head. "I tried that. Ask Oliver. It was a disaster. No one wanted to listen; everyone started fighting or disappeared."

"Did you go door-to-door?"

"No. I called a neighborhood meeting."

Leah nodded. Her husband was a good man, but years of working on his own and keeping an eye out for threats to his company dulled his people skills. "If we're going to band together as a community to survive this, we need to start small."

She walked toward the hall. "We have to convince people one at a time."

Grant stared at his wife. "You're amazing, you know that?"

Leah wished it were true. "I'm just afraid. It's a powerful motivator."

He nodded. "Be careful."

"You, too." Leah turned and headed down the stairs with Faith on her heels. She stopped in the kitchen and reassembled the trauma kit into the black backpack she'd put together years ago.

It had everything from Band-Aids to aspirin to QuikClot and emergency sutures. If anyone needed help in the neighborhood, she could deliver. First aid would go a long way to building trust.

At some point, she would have to refill or make more kits. A nasty gash would exhaust most of her bandages. A few burns, and she would need more ointment. But for now, it would do.

She slipped it onto her back and adjusted the straps before grabbing the air rifle. No sense in leaving herself completely defenseless. With the gun in her hand and the pack on her back, Leah was ready to bring the neighborhood together.

"Honey?"

Leah paused at the front door. "Yeah?"

Grant hustled after her. "You don't need to stop by Stan and Debbie's place."

"Why not?"

"They're dead."

Leah swallowed. "Do I need to know the details?"

"Half the neighborhood watched Stan die in the street."

She sucked in a breath. It was worse than she feared. "Did anyone help him?"

"I did."

Leah rushed up to her husband and kissed him quickly on the cheek. "Thank you."

"It was the right thing to do."

"So is this." She squeezed his arm. "I'll be back before dark."

"I will, too."

"You better be." Leah smiled one last time at her husband and tugged open the front door. The afternoon sun hit her face and she glanced down at Faith. "Ready to make some new friends?"

The little dog stared up at her, solemn and unsure.

"I'm scared, too. But we've got to take a chance. No one can stay an island forever."

CHAPTER THREE

LEAH

Rose Valley Lane
  Smyrna, Georgia
  Sunday, 3:00 p.m.

Leah checked her watch and stared down the street. Three hours until the sun would hug the tops of the houses. She wouldn't be able to get very far, but at least it would be a start. She glanced down the street in both directions, trying to decide where to go.

Stan and Debbie were out. Harvey next door didn't like dogs, so not a good first stop. But Becky and her husband Jeff two doors down might be a good choice. Leah headed that way with her shoulders back and a smile on her face.

The couple had moved in two years ago after they got married and had been friendly additions to the neighborhood. Leah walked up their short driveway and stopped at the front door. The shutters on the front of the house were closed.

Leah knocked on the door.

Faith whined at her feet and Leah glanced down. "It's okay. They like dogs."

No one answered. She knocked louder. "Becky? Jeff? Is anyone home?"

"They never came back."

Leah turned around. Jennifer's husband, Greg, stood in the middle of the street, arms folded across his chest. His barrel of a belly stuck out above his pants and his arms rested on top. He didn't smile.

She tried to keep her voice light. "How do you know?"

"They always go out Friday nights. Date night or something. Jeff was always gloating about it." Greg tipped his head toward the garage. "Cars aren't there, either."

Leah ran her tongue over her lower lip. There were no windows to a single garage in the neighborhood. If Greg knew it sat empty, either he broke in or found a way to manually lift the garage door to check. Neither option gave Leah the warm fuzzies.

Faith echoed her unease with a low growl and Leah bent down and rubbed her back.

"What's with the dog?"

"We adopted her."

Greg snorted. "Bad timing if you ask me."

I didn't. Leah exhaled. "How's Jennifer?"

"She's fine."

"And the boys?"

"Can't complain."

"Do you all need anything? First aid? Medicine?"

"Electricity would be damn nice. So would a hot meal or a cold beer. You got any of those?"

Leah's cheeks heated. "No. All out."

"Too bad." He lapsed into silence, but made no move to leave.

Leah hesitated. She never understood why Greg had taken a dislike to her and Grant, but whatever the problem, no matter how nice Leah was to Greg, he always had the same bad attitude.

She tried once more. "Do you know anyone who's sick? I've got a few supplies. I can try and make them comfortable."

"Doesn't look like you're very good at it."

Leah bit her tongue to keep from saying something mean. She knew her looks would be a problem, but Greg never gave her the benefit of the doubt. He always saw the worst in anything she or her husband did.

In the spring he'd complained about their tree encroaching on the street. In the fall, he complained about their leaf bags taking up too much space. In the winter, it was their fireplace stinking up the neighborhood.

He never gave them a moment's peace and Leah couldn't figure it out. She steeled herself and tried one last time to diffuse the hostility. "I know I look rough, but it's not easy to give yourself stitches without a suture kit.

Now that I'm home, I've got my supplies. Please, do you know anyone who needs help?"

"Other than Stan? Not a one. But I guess it's too late for him, isn't it?"

"I wasn't here."

"No, you weren't."

Leah exhaled. "Look, Greg, I don't know what your issue is with me or my husband, but I'm only trying to help."

"Take it somewhere else. We don't need it."

"But some of our neighbors might."

"Your husband sure would like that, wouldn't he? After his show the other night, getting up in front of everyone to tell us what to do and how to act." Greg shook his head and the disgust in his tone was plain. "He's not in charge around here anymore, no matter how much he wants to be."

Leah blinked. Was that what this was all about? She swallowed hard as a memory hit her. Way back when they first moved to the neighborhood, the builder held elections for the neighborhood homeowner's association. Grant ran against Greg and won.

But Grant hadn't served on the HOA board in years. At least five other neighbors had been elected since then. Leah swallowed. Had Greg let his resentment over losing fester this long?

She sucked in a breath. "I don't think Grant wants to be in charge of anything. He only wants to help. Just like I do."

The door to Greg's house opened and his wife called out. "Babe? Are you done? I need you inside."

Greg shouted into the street without turning around. "Be there in a minute."

"It's an emergency."

He scowled at Leah. "Stay out of our business."

Leah didn't say a word as Greg turned around. His wife, Jennifer, stood in the open doorway of their home, watching.

As they both disappeared inside, Leah finally exhaled. So far, she wasn't getting the warm welcome she expected. Maybe the next house would be better. She bent down to pet Faith. "How about we go to the Petersons' house? They've got little girls who would love to pet you."

She headed toward the end of the street with Faith by her side. As she stepped onto the Peterson's driveway, a slamming door caught her ear. Someone down Canary Avenue shouted.

Faith lowered into a crouch and flattened her ears. Leah walked to the corner, air rifle in her hand and ready.

As she crossed Rose Valley Lane and headed down Canary, another shout rang out and Leah could finally make out the words.

"You can't take that!"

Laughter echoed down the street. Leah glanced down at Faith. "I'm going to check it out. If you want to stay here, you can."

The little dog glanced up at her and growled. "I know, it sounds bad, but we can handle it."

Faith seemed to accept Leah's answer, tentatively advancing down the sidewalk, ears perked and listening. Leah followed, rifle gripped in both hands. She slowed as a pair of boys came into view.

Tall and lanky, with broad shoulders and spindly legs that grew faster than their muscles could, the pair were unmistakable. Greg's boys, David and Preston.

Leah ground her teeth together.

The pair had always been troublemakers. First riding their bikes all through the neighborhood when they were younger, right over Leah's flower bed by the mailbox and Debbie's day lilies. Then revving the engines of their dirt bikes at all hours and tearing down the middle of the street when little kids were out on the playground and in their yards.

The neighborhood association had fined Greg and his wife more than once, but it never seemed to change the boys' behavior. Now that Leah understood Greg's hostility a bit more, it made sense. He was bitter and taking it out on the entire neighborhood through his own actions and those of his boys.

Leah eased down the street, keeping to the edge of the houses to stay unobserved.

A woman Leah didn't know stood on her front lawn gesticulating at the brothers. "You can't just walk back there and steal my propane. I need that to cook!"

The older brother, David, held a propane tank with both arms. "So do we."

"Then find your own."

Preston laughed. "We did!"

Leah couldn't believe it. They were stealing a neighbor's propane tank? What on earth for? It wasn't like anyone could have any meat to cook at this point. A week without power and anything refrigerated or frozen was rotten.

She stepped forward. "If that isn't yours, you need to give it back."

Preston turned toward her voice. With a short spring haircut and a golf shirt on, he looked like the spitting image of his father. He recoiled as he looked her over. "What's it matter to you?"

"I care about right and wrong."

He scoffed. "Whatcha gonna do? Call the police?"

His brother joined in. "How you gonna get 'em here? Last time I checked there's no phones, lady. No cars. There aren't any rules anymore."

"Just because there aren't police doesn't mean there aren't laws. Stealing is a crime. You need to give that back."

"I don't need to do anything." David turned toward Leah and waggled the tank in his arms. "You gonna shoot me?"

She exhaled. There was no point in talking to the boys. They wouldn't change their minds because she asked them to. Her afternoon was going from hopeful to miserable and there was nothing she could do about it. Walking away wasn't an option.

If she let them take the propane tank, what would be next? Her truck? Someone else's food? Leah brought the rifle into position. "Wouldn't be the first time this week."

Preston's eyes widened and he eased closer to his brother. "David, come on, man. She's got a gun."

"She won't shoot me."

"You want to take that chance? One bullet in the center of that propane tank and the whole thing will explode. You'll be blasted into a million little pieces and so will your brother." Leah didn't even know if that was true, but it sounded scary, so she went with it.

David kept the bravado going, but his voice cracked when he spoke. "My dad will kill you for that."

"Funny, I ran into your dad just now. Does he know what you're doing?"

Preston shifted on his feet. "Put it down and let's go."

"No way. We need it."

"How about I turn around and go tell your dad what you're up to?"

"David, come on."

"Shut up, Preston. She's bluffing."

"What if I'm not?" Leah stepped closer, keeping her head bent on the sights of the rifle. "What if these are the last few moments of your life?"

CHAPTER FOUR

GRANT

2210 Canary Avenue
Smyrna, Georgia
Sunday 5:00 p.m.

Grant pushed up to stand. "It was worth a shot. Maybe we can try again tomorrow."

Oliver nodded. "I'll have to set up solar panels to charge the batteries, so maybe in the evening?"

It had been a frustrating few hours trying to access any part of the web with no success. Grant headed toward the door. "If you manage to get online tonight, come find me."

"Will do." Oliver remained hunched over his computer, trying in vain to reach out to the invisible world.

Grant let himself out the back door, locking the door

handle before pulling it shut. Like all the houses in the neighborhood, Oliver's backyard sported a concrete patio and a postage stamp bit of grass. No more than ten feet separated the houses, and the strips of land in the middle were full of gravel or mud or some combination of the two.

The perils of new developments. Every neighbor knew everyone else's business and fights with open windows carried several houses away. If Leah couldn't bring the neighborhood together, Grant worried what living on top of each other would mean for the future.

When your neighbor a handful of steps away was starving, would you share the last of your food? If someone down the street couldn't contribute to the community, would everyone still let that person stay?

The more Grant thought about it, the more unease soured his stomach. He ducked through the gate at Oliver's fence line and shut it behind him, wishing his fears would stay in the backyard.

As he hit the road, two things caught his attention: his wife with her air rifle in the middle of the street and Faith flat on her belly, snarling in his direction.

"You won't shoot me!"

Grant spun around. Greg's two good-for-nothing sons stood twenty feet away. One held a propane tank to his chest and the other looked like he was about to bolt.

Without another thought, Grant pulled his M&P Shield from its holster and ensured it was ready to fire. He brought it up with two hands and called out. "What the hell is going on?"

The kid with nothing in his hands jumped at the sight of the gun. "Shit, David. He's got a gun, too. Put it down! This is getting out of hand."

Leah called out. "He's stealing the propane tank."

"That's right." A voice Grant recognized called out. Grant tracked it to a woman ten or fifteen years his senior with curly short hair and overalls.

"Hey, Susie. Is that yours?"

She nodded.

"Then I don't see why you kids should have it."

"We need it." David, the one holding the tank, almost whined.

"Stealing isn't the answer."

"Then what is? It's not like the stores are open."

"Put it down." No teenagers were going to steal from their neighbors as long as Grant lived in the neighborhood. It wouldn't become a lawless free-for-all. Not yet.

He counted to five. "I'm not messing around."

At last, David set the tank on the asphalt.

Grant lowered the gun. "Get the hell out of here."

Preston balked. "You're not going to hurt us?"

"No. But don't try to steal anything from one of your neighbors ever again. Next time I won't be so lenient."

The boys took off, running as fast as their knobby knees could take them. Grant holstered the gun and walked over to his wife. "We've got to stop meeting like this."

Leah smiled, but the strain of the encounter pulled the corners of her mouth down. "Tell me about it."

Faith head-butted his shin and he bent down to pat her head.

Susie called out to them. "Thank you both."

Grant tugged Leah toward Susie's house and the pair stopped in her driveway. He smiled. "It's the least we could do."

Susie hurried over to pick up the propane tank and carry it back to her house. "I can't believe you stood up to them."

"Why?"

"They're Greg's boys. He's liable to have a problem with it."

Leah shuddered. "I ran into Greg outside. He's got a problem with everything."

Grant raised an eyebrow. "What happened?"

"Let's just say he's not the friendliest neighbor."

"Well, I am." Susie motioned toward her house. "I've got some sun tea that's ready on the back porch. Want to come over for a while?"

"Can Faith come?"

Susie glanced down at the little dog. "Of course."

"Then we'd love to. Tea sounds great."

Grant followed Leah into the older woman's house. Where their place was minimal and almost modern, Susie's was full of color and fabric. Candles dotted every table and artwork adorned every wall.

He could almost forget her floor plan was the same as his own. Susie ushered them out to her backyard where a pergola covered the concrete patio that she'd painted a rich brown. She set the propane tank back on the shelf beneath the grill.

Grant broke the silence. "Thanks for inviting us over."

Leah agreed. "You're the first neighbor who hasn't either wanted to steal from me or chastise me for trying to help."

Susie poured tea from a glass pitcher and motioned for them to sit down. She glanced at Leah's head with a question in her eyes.

Grant patted his wife on the arm. "Unfortunately, she wasn't auditioning for a zombie flick when the world ended."

"Then what happened?"

Leah reached up and touched her head. "How about I start at the beginning? It'll make more sense that way."

Grant listened while his wife filled both him and Susie in on her past week, everything from her trials at the hospital to Dr. Phillips and their escape from downtown. The bookstore where she waited out the worst of the fallout. The Walmart and the men she helped. Then the car crash and the head wound and the vicious cat, followed by a kind old woman and a terrible hospital experience.

Grant marveled.

His wife had more strength than he ever knew she possessed. How she left her sister behind and set off to find him without even spending the night in Hampton to rest up was beyond him. With a head wound and an infection and only an air rifle for defense, she managed to traverse almost a hundred miles when most of their neighbors never even left their street.

Susie leaned back in her chair. "That's incredible. I can't believe you went through all that." She glanced at Grant. "I knew your husband had it rough at the sporting goods store, but all those dead people in the hospital..." Susie shuddered.

"What sporting goods store?" Leah focused on Grant and waited.

Grant indulged her curiosity and told his own story of the past week. He confirmed that downtown was nothing but a crater and that people were already turning away from the rule of law. He glossed over the shootout, but Susie chimed in.

"That's not the way Dan tells it. He says you were a regular cowboy out there, standing up to eight guys with nothing but a handgun. He said you were lucky to make it out alive."

Leah's eyes went wide.

"Dan exaggerates. Did he tell you he had two rifles to back me up? Or that he shot first?"

Susie shook her head.

"Didn't think so."

Leah reached out and squeezed Grant's hand. "I'm glad you made it out safely."

"So am I." Grant drained the rest of his tea and set the empty glass on the table. "But between the men at the strip mall, Donny the other night, and now Greg's boys, I don't have a lot of confidence in our fellow man."

Susie's face fell. "You think it's going to get worse?"

"I know it is."

"What should we do?"

Grant ran a hand through his hair and glanced up at the setting sun. "I have no idea. There are eighty-seven houses in our neighborhood. How many of those would actually join forces?"

Leah shook her head. "Not as many as I thought, I'm afraid."

Susie agreed. "From what I've seen the last few days, it might be everyone for themselves." She pulled a sweater off the back of her chair and slipped it on. "No one wants to share. No one wants to admit that they need help. It's like the bombs killed more than people. They killed our spirit."

"I don't believe that." Leah thumped the table. "We can't be the only people in the neighborhood who want to work together."

Grant opened his mouth to argue when a tremendous hammering on Susie's front door sent Faith into a frenzy. She rushed into the house, barking loud enough to drown out the person outside.

With his hand out to caution Susie and Leah to wait, Grant rose up and eased into the house. He pulled his gun from the holster and held it pointed to the floor as he approached.

After looking through the peephole, he yanked open the front door. Dan stood on the front step, panting and out of breath.

"What's going on?"

"It's...your...truck." He clutched the doorframe for support.

"The one Leah drove here? What about it?"

Dan sucked in another lungful of air. "It's on fire."

CHAPTER FIVE

GRANT

2078 Rose Valley Lane
   Smyrna, Georgia
   Sunday, 7:00 p.m.

The smell of burning rubber wrinkled Grant's nose a full minute before the flames forced him to a stop. Dan was right.

Flames lapped over the hood of Leah's truck, flicking and licking the air like red and orange snakes. Noxious plumes of gray smoke turned the dusk to night. Grant coughed as he inhaled the dirty air.

They had only been gone a few hours. Why would someone set fire to one of the few working vehicles in the neighborhood? Didn't they know the value of a truck for hauling food and supplies?

He spun around, searching for anything to put out

the flames. A fire hydrant sat three houses away, but without the tools to open it, it was useless. No one owned a pool and even if he could find a bucket, it would be too little, too late.

As the fire engulfed the bench seat, flames leaped into the air. Embers landed hot and glowing on the concrete. If a bit of burning fabric hit their roof...

Grant rushed toward the fire, skirting the edge of the heat to reach the garage. Flames singed the air off his forearm and he stumbled back.

Dan lumbered across the next-door neighbor's driveway, face red as a cherry and soaked in sweat. He stopped in the strip of grass separating the houses. "Do you have a hose?"

Grant nodded. "In the garage, but it's too hot to get the big door open. I'll have to go through the house."

"Hurry."

Grant ran around the truck as giant, billowing clouds of black smoke filled the sky. He fumbled with the keys before stumbling into the dark house. The fire lit up the entryway like a horror movie, casting shadows ten feet tall and wide.

After tearing down the hall and into the kitchen, he yanked open the interior door to the garage. As a blast of hot air smacked his face, he recoiled.

The heat from the fire turned the garage into an oven. Without insulation on the exterior door, the metal acted as a giant electrical coil, baking the inside of the garage. He rushed to the wire shelving.

The shelf full of fertilizer and lawn chemicals sat eye level. Even in the near-darkness, he could make out the warning labels. They had to contain the fire before something in the garage exploded.

If the house caught on fire, everything they owned would be destroyed. They would have nothing. How could they survive the coming months without food or shelter or supplies?

Grant dug through the bottom shelf until he found the hose in the dark. Reversing his steps, he rushed back out to the water spigot.

Dan waited beside it. "Hook it up and turn it wide open. I'll douse the house. If it stays wet enough, it won't catch."

Grant crouched to attach the hose and turned the water on. Before the EMP and the bombs, their water pressure was strong enough to ruin landscaping and blow dirt out of cracks in the driveway. Now the water dribbled out of the hose in a limp stream.

"Is that it?"

Grant nodded.

Dan grimaced as he stretched the hose closer to the house. "Do you have a fire extinguisher?"

"Never got around to it." Grant cursed his foolishness. He knew the risks. A grease fire in the kitchen. Hot lawn clippings in a sealed bag in the sun. All sorts of ordinary events could cause a fire, but he'd never taken the extra step to prepare.

"I don't have one either, but you need to find one.

Even if I keep the water running, it won't be enough to save the house if the fire gets much bigger."

Dan pointed the hose at the siding around the garage door and the roof, soaking everything he could reach. Grant rushed back to the street. The flames consumed his night vision, plunging all but the most immediate houses into darkness. For all he knew, half the block stood down the street, watching in silent horror.

He looked around with wide eyes. Where were his neighbors? Why was no one trying to help them? As he ran into the street, two shapes materialized out of the dark.

Leah and Susie.

They each held a fire extinguisher in their hands.

Grant exhaled. In the rush to reach his house, he hadn't stopped to talk to his wife or ask for help. He'd only reacted.

She ran up to him, eyes reflecting the worst of the flames. "Who would do this?"

"I have no idea." He glanced back at the truck, now fully engulfed. "We can't salvage the truck, but we need to put the fire out before the house catches. The garage is way over a hundred degrees inside."

Susie pulled the pin on the fire extinguisher. "I'll work on the front of the truck. Leah, you hit the back."

Grant looked around in a panic as the women moved toward the truck. "Where's Faith?"

"Back at Susie's. We left her there in case this was really bad."

Grant nodded as Susie depressed the lever on her extinguisher. A blanket of white foam landed on the hood of the truck and smothered the flames. She worked it back and forth like a sprinkler, concentrating on the space between the windshield and the metal.

The flames receded and Grant hurried back to help Dan. The older man stood beside the truck, pointing the hose at the house with a grimace.

"What's the matter?" Grant reached for the hose.

Dan stumbled back. His entire left arm was covered in angry welts. "Got a little too close to the truck. The flames were coming this way, so I tried to beat them back with the water." He winced. "They got me instead."

"As soon as we're able, get inside and let Leah treat you. We've got to have something to take care of that."

Dan nodded, his face streaked with soot and pain.

"Can you make it to Susie's and Oliver's?"

"I don't see why not. My arm's burned, not my feet."

Grant grinned despite the situation. "Can you get my dog Faith and Oliver and bring them here?"

"Why? That kid wouldn't know how to put out a fire unless it was on the internet."

"He needs to know what's happening."

Dan nodded and set off down the street and in moments, he was lost to the darkness.

Thanks to Susie and Leah's work with the fire extinguishers, the worst of the flames died down. Grant turned from soaking the house to the truck. It didn't take long to contain the rest of the fire.

As the last of the smoke slowed to a wisp, he sagged against the wet wall of the house.

Leah came over and joined him, sweat dripping off her nose. She wiped it away. "That was close. If Dan hadn't seen the fire..."

"Tell me about it."

Leah leaned back against the house and closed her eyes. "Why didn't anyone come to help us?"

"Guess we didn't win the popularity contest."

Susie dropped the empty fire extinguisher on the lawn and came over to join them.

"Thank you for helping."

"Of course. Why wouldn't I?"

Grant scrubbed his face. "You could ask everyone else in the neighborhood the same thing."

Susie glanced around. "It *is* late. Maybe they didn't know."

Grant snorted. "That fire was the brightest thing for miles. Everyone knew."

"They're a bunch of pathetic limp noodles. That's why." Dan grunted as he deposited Faith at Grant's feet.

Oliver hurried up the driveway, side-eyeing the burnt-out truck the entire way. "I guess I missed all the fun."

"Something like that." Grant bent to scratch Faith behind the ear. The dog ducked behind his legs and stared out at the street. She knew the fire meant trouble, too. He motioned to Leah. "Dan's got a burn on his arm. Can you treat it?"

Leah pushed off the wall in an instant. "Of course. If

the fire's out, how about we come inside and I can check everyone for injuries?"

Susie turned to stare at the street. "Are you sure it's safe?"

"The truck's a cinder. With all the foam and water bogging it down, there's no way it will re-ignite."

"What about the house?"

Grant weighed the odds. "I'm guessing whoever lit the truck on fire is done for the night. If they really wanted to hurt us, whoever did it would have set fire to the house. So far, they aren't that bold."

"So far? What else has happened?" Oliver pushed his glasses up his nose and stared at the truck.

"Come on in and we can discuss it. I don't want to talk out here."

Grant opened the door and everyone filed in past him.

Leah paused on the step with Faith at her heels. "Do you really think we're okay to not guard the front of the house?"

His brow pinched as he thought it over. "Yes and no, to be honest. But we can't figure out what to do if we're too busy staring out into the dark." He glanced down at Faith. "She'll let us know if someone is poking around."

"Are you sure?"

"About her?" Grant smiled down at the dog as she walked into the house and took up position by the front door. "Definitely."

Leah exhaled. "All right. Then I'll treat Dan and anyone else who needs help."

"And together we'll figure out what the hell is going on."

Grant followed his wife inside and shut the door. Faith lingered by the front of the house, ears alert and listening.

CHAPTER SIX

LEAH

2078 Rose Valley Lane
  Smyrna, Georgia
  Sunday, 10:00 p.m.

The skin on Dan's arm puckered with blisters, but as Leah applied a salve, she smiled. "It's a mild second-degree. A few of the blisters might weep or ooze, but as long as you keep it bandaged and clean, it should heal in a couple of weeks."

"Thanks." Dan glanced up and Leah followed his gaze. Her husband paced the kitchen in the dark, head bent in thought.

Dan called out. "You keep doing that and the wood floor will wear straight through. You'll be walking on concrete slab before you know it."

Grant slowed. "I think better when I walk."

Leah finished bandaging Dan's arm and stood up.

Susie and Oliver sat at the breakfast table with Dan, sharing a lantern and each other's company. Leah met her husband in the kitchen. "Is it the fire? Or something else?"

He rubbed the back of his neck and his frown deepened. "I think we need to leave."

"What?"

"We should pack our things and hit the road."

Leah shook her head. "And go where?"

Grant ground his fist into his palm. "Anywhere. There are a million small towns that escaped the nuclear bombs. One of them will let us in."

Leah crossed her arms. "I'm not going to Hampton."

"I didn't say that. We could go anywhere."

"What does a small town have that we don't?"

Grant threw up his hands and walked into the breakfast area. "You all see it, don't you? We have to get out of here."

Susie balked. "Leave my home? Why? I've got a place to sleep and a small garden. If I convert the rest of the backyard, I can live off what I grow."

"You really think your neighbors will let you do that?"

She leaned back in her chair and glanced at Dan.

The big man grunted as he moved his injured arm. "Don't see how leaving is going to help us."

"If we get out of the city, we can find a place where it's still life as usual."

Oliver snorted. "Good luck. Nowhere has any power. Without electricity, it's not normal life anywhere."

"There's got to be some, somewhere." Grant pointed at Oliver. "You've got solar panels. When I was trying to get home, I ran across a farm totally off the grid. They had all the electricity they needed."

Leah couldn't believe the words out of her husband's mouth. Leave their home? She looked around. Everything she owned was sitting all around them.

They bought the breakfast table with her first paycheck as a nurse. The rug in the living room came from a trip to India her mother had taken before she died. The pictures on the wall were of their wedding.

Grant wanted to pack up and leave it all behind? She pressed her fingers against her lips and thought it over. She didn't have any faith that another community would let them in or treat them any better than Hampton. "What about the farmer? Would he accept us?"

"No." Grant shook his head. "He made that pretty clear."

Leah focused on the floor. "Then we should stay and make the best of it. Help our neighbors."

Grant jabbed a finger toward the front door. "You mean the ones who set the truck on fire? We should help *those people?*"

Susie spoke up. "We don't know who set the fire."

"She's right. For all we know, it was someone just passing through."

"Then why didn't anyone offer to help?"

"Maybe they were afraid."

"Or maybe they were complicit." Grant turned to Dan. "You have to see my point."

After a moment, Dan nodded. "I do."

"Thank God."

"But I don't know if we should leave."

Grant opened his mouth, but Leah held up a hand. "Listen to him, honey. Please."

Dan flashed her a tight smile and eased closer to the table. "Susie is right. We don't know who started the fire. It could have been Greg or his boys, or it could have been someone we least expect."

"What's your point?"

"We need to figure out who our enemies are before we make any decisions. If the whole neighborhood is against us, do you really think they'll just let us leave?"

"If we leave now, they won't have a chance to stop us."

"How do you propose we do that?" Dan shook his head. "We lost our only means of transportation."

Grant resumed pacing. "I've got Stan's motorcycle."

"Okay, so there's room for one, maybe two if you squeeze. But what about the rest of us?"

"We could walk."

Oliver spoke up for the first time. "And get ambushed by those guys from the sporting goods store? No, thank you. I'd rather take my chances here."

"We can find a car. I've done it once, I can do it again."

"But in the meantime, we need to stay put." Leah reached out as her husband approached and stilled him with a hand. She knew he meant well, but they couldn't run away at the first sign of trouble.

"Leah's right." Dan focused on his injured arm. "Until we're forced to go, I say we stay and make the most of it. We can always prepare so that we're ready."

Grant ran a hand down his face. "No one wants to leave?"

Leah looked at their three neighbors. Each one of them shook their heads. She smiled at her husband. "We're not saying never. We're just saying not yet." She squeezed his arm. "We still have a chance to help people here. I don't want to waste that because we're afraid."

Her husband took her hand. "I don't want you to get hurt because you didn't know when to give up."

"There's no guarantee we won't be hurt on the road. Even after the fire, our house is our safest bet."

"What if next time it's not a truck? What if it's the house?" Grant looked past Leah to the front door. "Or Faith?"

Leah turned toward the little fluff ball. "If anyone lays a hand on her, I'll be the first to give them hell. But until then, we should try and work it out."

"I think it's a mistake."

"But you'll stay?"

Leah waited as her husband struggled with the issue. She understood his need to protect her and his sincerity in thinking leaving was the best strategy. But it was instinct talking. If they were going to leave, they needed transportation and a plan.

If they walked out of the neighborhood with nothing but what they could carry, it would end in disaster. At a minimum, they needed food, water, and a destination.

Wandering north through Smyrna and on into Marietta or Alpharetta would do nothing but exhaust their supplies and their bodies.

They needed to hold on to what they had unless push came to shove. Only then would she be willing to go. She opened her mouth to say as much when Grant's shoulders sagged.

"Fine. We'll stay. But I want to be ready in case we have to evacuate. Bags packed and by the door."

"Deal." Leah dropped her hand and sucked in a breath. Staying meant she could check on the other neighbors down the street and treat any injuries. Maybe if she helped enough people, whoever set the fire would see the error of their ways.

She rubbed her arms. Now that the truck was ashes and warped metal, the cold night air even dropped the temperature inside the house. Summer was coming, but not fast enough.

Yet another reason not to rush out the door. How would they survive without shelter? Even if they made it through the summer months, if they didn't secure somewhere safe and warm by winter, they were setting themselves up for sickness and even hypothermia.

She shuddered just thinking it over. Her husband draped a sweater over her shoulders. She smiled at him. "Thank—"

A low growl from across the first floor cut Leah off. Even in the dim light, she could make out Faith's stark white form at the door. The dog growled again.

Grant pulled his handgun from his holster. Dan rose

up, but Grant waved him off. "Stay and rest your arm. I'll check it out."

"Be careful." Leah watched as her husband crept out of the kitchen toward the front door. He crouched in the dark beside Faith, more a ghost than a person.

Susie reached out and took Leah's hand. "It's probably nothing."

Leah didn't respond. From what little she'd seen of Faith so far and what Grant told her about the dog, Leah knew it wasn't nothing. If Faith growled, someone was outside.

With a lungful of air trapped in her throat, she waited as Grant unlocked the door. He disappeared into the night and Faith darted out with him.

An agonizing few minutes later, both returned. Grant carried a piece of paper into the breakfast area. He tossed it onto the table beside the light.

Leah leaned in to read it.

Attention All Residents
Mandatory Community Meeting
Monday 9:00 a.m., Clubhouse
Bring an inventory of all food and water, first aid, and
vehicles
No Weapons Allowed

She glanced up at her husband.

He still held his gun in one hand and a scowl on his face.

"Did you see who dropped it off?"

"No." Grant pointed at the paper. "And that isn't our copy of the invitation."

"It isn't?" Dread iced Leah's spine.

"No. Every front door got one taped to it but ours."

"Where did it come from?"

"Stan and Debbie's place. No one knows she's dead but me."

Susie gasped. "Debbie's gone?"

Grant nodded. "She killed herself. I found her lying beside Stan in their bed."

"Oh my God." Susie brought a hand up to her mouth.

Oliver paled.

Dan pushed back his chair and stood up. "Looks like it's going to be a long night."

CHAPTER SEVEN

LEAH

Neighborhood Clubhouse
   Smyrna, Georgia
   Monday, 9:00 a.m.

Neighbors from the entire development streamed down the street like ants following a trail. Here and there, a few people she knew cast looks Leah's way. She couldn't tell if they were surprised because they knew they weren't invited, or because her husband had called the first meeting.

That morning, Grant had filled her in on how badly everything went down a few days before, with some in the neighborhood calling for confiscation of weapons and food and Grant shouting them down. If today was anything like the prior meeting, she would have to keep an eye on her husband.

The thought of handing anything over wouldn't sit

well with Grant. Not that she liked it, either, but Leah preferred to disagree with silence rather than a shouting match.

Leah hugged Grant's arm as they approached the clubhouse. "You're sure about this?"

"Coming to the meeting? Of course. We need to know what's going on."

"But the flyer."

"I'm not letting these people push us around." Grant forced a smile as they ducked inside.

A giant sign proclaiming *No Weapons* was handwritten and taped to the clubhouse door. Grant didn't even pause even though Leah knew he was armed. No sense in arguing with the man when he had a point.

She was willing to give people the benefit of the doubt, but only so far. After the past week, going anywhere without a weapon or her husband was a recipe for disaster. Leah eased through the crowd in Grant's wake.

The room was at capacity and beyond, with neighbors brushing shoulders just to find a place to stand. Ducking into the rear corner, Leah tried to blend in.

She checked the knit cap she'd pulled from the closet and confirmed it hid her wound. Wearing a winter hat in March was a little odd, but having people stare at her bald head and wound was worse.

Next to her stood one of their neighbors from across the street. As Leah smiled at her, the woman's eyes went wide. She stepped away.

Leah reached for Grant's hand.

"What? Is something wrong?"

She leaned in to whisper. "I don't think we're welcome here."

"Of course we aren't." He pretended like she'd said something funny and smiled. "Just act like you have no idea why. Make whoever is out to get us be the jerk here."

"What happened to all of your anger from last night?"

He smiled again. "I can't flush out our enemies if I'm causing a scene."

Leah shook her head and pretended to laugh. "You sound like a tough guy in a movie."

"I'm being realistic."

"What's so funny?" Susie made it through the crowd to stand in the now-empty space beside Leah.

"People are avoiding us."

"Wouldn't call that laugh-worthy." Dan huffed out a breath as he filled up the rest of the gap. Holding his wounded arm bent by his side, he surveyed the sea of people. "You all ready for this?"

"As ready as we'll ever be." Grant patted Leah's hand.

She sucked in a breath as a man she didn't recognize climbed up on top of the fireplace hearth.

"Hello, everyone. Thank you for coming." Raising up on his tiptoes, the man shouted above the din of conversations.

The room quieted.

"For those of you who don't know me, I'm Will Greene. I live on Canary." With his blond hair and easy-going smile, he could have been an actor in a toothpaste commercial.

Leah leaned toward Susie. "I don't know him."

"He's new." Susie whispered back. "Only moved in a few months ago. Has a wife, no kids."

"Over the past few days, I've had a chance to speak to most of the neighborhood and it's clear there's a consensus on our next steps."

Grant stiffened. Leah squeezed his hand.

"In order to make the most of the coming days and weeks, we need to pool our resources and come together as a community. Aid will be coming. Hopefully, the power along with it. But until then, we need to unite."

Grant snorted and Leah yanked on his arm to be quiet. She focused on Will and his orange polo shirt. Maybe he would have a sensible plan.

"We'll start with converting the clubhouse here into a pantry and supply facility."

Leah nodded. Sensible plan. They could gather more food from the nearby stores and ration it out here.

"Everyone, please deliver your list of food and weapons to Greg. We have a neighborhood directory and once we receive your list, we will cross you off. Tomorrow we'll begin going door-to-door to collect."

Will smiled as Greg, their obnoxious neighbor across the street, held up his hand.

Leah swallowed. There was nothing sensible about confiscation. She ran her tongue across her lips. Surely someone else in the room objected, didn't they? She looked around her.

Everyone stood like sheeple, nodding and unfolding pieces of paper covered in handwritten lists. They queued up in line and muted conversations filled the space once more.

Beside her, Susie pulled out a folded note.

"What are you doing?"

She glanced up at Leah, confused. "Pulling out my inventory."

"Are you giving it to them? Why?"

"I—" Susie paused. "I guess I don't really know."

Dan took the piece of paper and crumpled it in his fist. "You're not giving them a damn thing. Not now, not ever."

"But what about our neighbors?"

Dan exhaled and lowered his voice. "Think of it like an airplane crash. You put your oxygen mask on first before helping anyone else. We can help, but not if we're starving."

"Or defenseless." Grant pulled his hand out of Leah's embrace. "Someone should stop this."

Leah leaned into him. "I can go ask a few questions."

"I don't want you up there with Greg."

"He won't do anything with all these people here." Leah ducked away from Grant before he could pull her back.

Easing through the line with apologies every few steps, Leah reached the front. She checked to make sure her hat hid the gash on her head before smiling up at Will. "Hi, I don't think we've met. I'm Leah Walton."

"Will Greene." He shook her hand. "Nice to meet you."

"I just got back home after a few days on the road, so this is the first I'm hearing about the lists and the pantry. Can you explain what's going on?"

He smiled again, even wider. "Of course. Bunch of us got together and after talking it out, we decided that the easiest way to ensure we all have enough to eat and everyone is taken care of is to pool our resources."

She smiled wide enough to match Will. "That's wonderful, how you want to help out and all, but... what about finding a store with inventory? We could fill the clubhouse with food we've picked up instead of our neighbors' pantries."

Will's face fell, but he recovered quickly. "I don't think anywhere's open for business right now."

"Have you looked?"

He pulled on the collar of his shirt and glanced at Greg. The man was busy flipping pages of the directory and crossing off names.

"And about the weapons—you said those are being confiscated, too?"

"I wouldn't call it *confiscating*. More like, keeping them secure."

"Who gets to take them out?"

"Um... well... that hasn't really been decided yet."

Leah smiled. "So it is confiscation, then. You're taking them and not giving them back."

Will took a step back. "Look, now isn't really the time to get into any of this. If you have questions, I'm sure we can talk about it at your place or some other time."

Leah closed the distance between them and raised her voice. "You mean you don't want to answer the tough questions in front of all of our neighbors."

Will glanced around. "I don't want to distract from the purpose of the meeting."

"To take everyone's food and defenses so that we're helpless. Because that's what this is really about, isn't it?"

Will's mouth opened and shut like a fish and the conversations behind Leah trickled off into silence.

Greg shouted over the crowded line. "Is there a problem here?"

Leah turned to him. "I have questions about who is going to distribute the food. I have questions about who is going to police the weapons and whether anyone is going to be able to get them back."

"We've already decided."

"Who decided? Was there a vote I missed?"

Greg sneered. "It's not our fault you weren't home."

"So I shouldn't have tried to save lives at the hospital downtown? Or tried to get as many people to shelter as possible before the bomb? Or waited out the radiation plume before finally setting off?" Leah's voice rose with every question, her words coming out clipped and short.

"Your decision, not mine."

She opened her mouth to say something more, but a hand wrapped around her wrist. Grant leaned close enough to whisper. "Let it go, honey."

Leah fumed. Everything Grant had warned about

was coming to pass. Even with the truck fire, she hadn't believed him. She hadn't been willing to think so little of their neighbors. People who had lived beside them for years.

"That's right, Grant. You tell that wife of yours she's out of line."

Whoa. Leah yanked her hand away from Grant and pushed through the crowd. She stopped in front of Greg. "Excuse me?"

He smirked. "You heard me. I made sure to shout."

"I don't know what your problem is, but we've done nothing to you." She jabbed her index finger an inch from his chest. "We deserve a say in what goes on in this neighborhood as much as the next person."

Greg snorted and glanced down at Leah's hand. "I'd step back if I were you."

"Or what?"

His eyes narrowed as his gaze settled back on her face. "Or I'll make you."

CHAPTER EIGHT

GRANT

Neighborhood Clubhouse
   Smyrna, Georgia
   Monday, 10:00 a.m.

Oh, hell no. Grant pulled his Shield from his holster and brandished it in a sweeping arc.

The nearest neighbors balked. A woman bumped into a pair of men. A man pushed two others aside. Shouts rose from all around.

"Gun!"

"Run!"

"Get out of here!"

Grant wanted to join in and tell them to hurry it up already. The path between him and Leah teemed with bodies. Shooting his neighbors was the last thing he wanted, but no one was going to threaten his wife.

"Clear the room!" Dan's voice boomed above the commotion. "Everyone out! Now!"

The no-nonsense tone pushed people into action. Arms shoved, heads ducked, and lists fell to the ground. Chaos. The crowd swelled at the double doors, undulating in a panicked wave as people rushed out into the morning light.

Grant wished there had been another way, but he had to protect his wife.

After a few moments, the space cleared. Five men were left standing around Greg and Will. Three he'd seen before down at the pool. All young, single, and probably eager for some authority. The other two he didn't know. If they were all part of Greg's posse, getting out of the clubhouse could be a problem.

He motioned to Leah. "Step out of the way, hon."

She stalked back behind him and Grant leveled the gun at Greg's chest.

"No one speaks to Leah that way. Not now, not ever."

Greg held up his hands like it was no big deal. "I'm not the one who brought a gun to a no-weapons-allowed event."

"I'm not the one who lit my truck on fire."

Greg's eyes narrowed.

"How about we just put the weapons away and have a conversation?" Will stood off to the side, wearing the same ridiculous grin he'd used at the beginning of the meeting.

Grant turned to Will. "So is this some sort of good-cop, bad-cop shakedown? Is that how you plan to run things?"

The man's smile faltered. "I don't know what you're talking about."

"*Mm-hmm.* And I've never watched a single episode of *The Walking Dead*. We're basically standing in ground zero for the new city of Alexandria right now and the two of you appointed yourselves the de facto leaders."

"This is nothing like that."

Dan eased up to Grant's side. "Seems pretty spot on to me. First you take everyone's food. Then you take away their ability to defend themselves. Then what? You decide who gets what and when?"

He shook his head. "How soon before you're shoving your face full of someone else's crackers and drinking their wine?"

Will crossed his arms. "We're doing this to help our neighbors, not steal from them."

Leah rolled her eyes. "If you wanted to help, then you'd find a working vehicle, assemble a team and go find a store that hasn't been ransacked. You wouldn't confiscate from the very people you claim to be helping."

The men between Will and Greg eyed Leah, Grant, and the rest of their friends with hooded eyes. Each one stared at them like they were assessing the odds and waiting for the right opportunity.

It didn't matter how much they argued, Will was never going to listen to reason. From the way he stared at them, to his defensive body language, it seemed he really did believe his own hype.

Greg, on the other hand... He knew exactly what he was doing and why.

Grant brought the attention back to him. "Will might have good intentions, but everyone knows you don't. You're only here to ensure you're in charge."

Greg didn't even open his mouth. Instead, he busied himself with picking up the lists people had dropped on the floor.

"You should know who you're teaming up with, Will." Grant turned to the other man. "Greg's kids tried to steal a propane tank from Susie yesterday, and someone, most likely Greg himself, set fire to our truck last night."

"You don't have any proof of that." Greg stood up with a stack of papers in his hand. "It could have been anyone on the street or a stranger looking for some fun."

"Or the neighbor who's had it out for us for years." Leah shook her head. "You did it. And you were the reason we weren't invited today."

Greg glanced around. "Looks like that was the right decision if you ask me."

Oliver and Susie hung back in the rear of the clubhouse. Grant motioned for them to head for the door. One of the men he didn't know moved to intercept them.

Grant aimed his gun on the man. "I don't think you want to start that battle."

The man glanced at Will.

After a moment, their leader shook his head. "Let them go. We don't need to keep them here." He frowned at Grant. "It's obvious they don't share our values."

Oliver and Susie scurried out the door, but Dan stayed by Grant's side. He nodded at the man by the door. "Hey, Logan. Didn't expect to see you at this meeting."

The other man managed a taut rise of his shoulders. "Don't see why not."

"You aren't much for rule-following, that's all." Dan glanced around. "But maybe you're hoping to be the one making the rules, is that it?"

Will held up his hands. "No one is here because they want to make the rules."

"Speak for yourself." Grant pointed his gun at Greg. "I know that's exactly why he's here."

Greg took a step, but Grant shook his head. "Don't give me a reason."

"How about we all just agree to disagree for now, okay?" Will motioned toward the door. "You can go and talk this over at home. We can start our inventory."

"And if we decide not to contribute?" Leah focused on Greg. "What happens then?"

"I'm sure we can come to an understanding." Will smiled at Leah, but it looked pained. "If we're through—"

Grant lowered his weapon but didn't put it away. "Stay away from our house and everyone else's who stuck around here. If anything happens to them, I'll hold you all responsible."

Will opened his mouth, but shut it after glancing at Greg.

Leah and Dan eased toward the door and Grant followed behind. He kept his focus trained on the clubhouse until they rounded the street corner and it was blocked from view.

Leah reached for him. "I'm sorry. That was all my fault."

"No, it wasn't. They're the ones to blame."

"If I'd kept my mouth shut—"

"You'd be furious at yourself." Grant holstered the Shield and gave his wife a sideways hug. "Your backbone is one of the reasons I love you."

Dan cleared his throat. "How about we save the mushy stuff for later, huh? We've got to find Oliver and Susie and come up with a plan."

Leah leaned past Grant. "What do you mean?"

"Seems pretty obvious. Even if we could have stayed before, we can't now. Greg will never stop. If we want to keep our wits and our gear, we need to leave."

Grant hustled up his driveway and found Susie and Oliver waiting in their rocking chairs on the front porch. Susie stood up when he came into view. "Are you all okay?"

Leah smiled and rushed up to give the older woman a hug. "We're fine. Sorry I got us in such a mess."

"If you want to blame someone, blame Greg." Oliver almost spat out the man's name in disgust. "He's the reason we're here."

"We should talk about this inside." Grant unlocked the door and Faith darted out. She slinked between everyone's legs, saying hello with tail wags and sniffs of jeans.

Grant reached down and gave her a pat as everyone

filed into the house. He turned on two lanterns and set them on the dining room table as each person found a seat.

Dan spoke first. "Like I told Grant and Leah on the walk back, it's obvious now that Greg will never leave us alone. And with the confiscation of all our food and any weapons we own, we'll never be safe if we stay here."

Grant nodded. "After the truck, I knew we had to go, but listening to Will this morning confirms it. Even if they don't go after us physically, they can make our lives miserable. If we don't give up our food and defenses, they'll come for us."

He motioned at Oliver and Susie. "Once they find out about your electronics and your garden, they'll take over. You won't have any control."

Leah pulled her legs up to her chest and sat sideways in the dining room chair. "Even after the truck, I thought we could stay. I thought there had to be an explanation. It couldn't just be animosity or fear. But I was wrong."

She focused on Grant and he smiled in encouragement. "Greg hates us. He's never going to stop until we're either broken or under his thumb. I don't want to stick around to find out how he's going to do it."

Susie rubbed her temples. "I agree that leaving makes the most sense, but where do we go? Does anyone own any land?"

Dan scratched his head. "There's a hunting lodge I've been to a few times up north of here. They've got hundreds of acres. We might be able to camp there for a while."

"My sister lives in Hampton, but I'm not sure if I'm ready to go back there."

Grant reached for Leah and took her hand. "Neither am I."

Oliver spoke up for the first time. "I've got an idea. It's not out in the country, but it's away from the blast area and Greg and his cronies won't follow us."

"Where?"

"Kennesaw State University."

"A college?" Dan scoffed. "Aren't we all a little old to be going back to school?"

Oliver put up a hand. "Hear me out. It's got a huge communications department with a radio station and a digital media lab. If anyone can connect to the outside world, they can."

Leah perked up. "It also has a nursing program. I could rebuild my trauma pack and fortify it with more supplies."

Grant nodded. "They also have a crisis preparation course. One of the guys I work with took it last year. If the college is operational, they might be able to help us."

Oliver glanced around the table. "So it's settled? We pack up and go?"

Grant nodded. "Everyone go home and assemble your gear. We can meet back here as soon as you're ready. Kennesaw State here we come."

CHAPTER NINE

GRANT

2078 Rose Valley Lane
Smyrna, Georgia
Monday, 4:00 p.m.

Grant stared at the two backpacks, massive pile of clothes, kitchen items, garage bits and pieces and more with a frown. "There is no way we can carry all of this."

Leah sat on the floor, struggling with a stuff sack and an uncooperative sleeping bag. "We've barely scratched the surface. There's a million more things we could take if we had the space."

"That's the thing. We don't have any space. We might be able to take a single backpack on the motorcycle or rig up some saddle bags, but with Faith, we can't put anything on the back."

Leah stared at him for a moment. "We can't take the

motorcycle. There's Dan, and Susie, and Oliver to think about. What are they going to do, run alongside?"

Grant rubbed his forehead. "But it will get us there so much faster."

"We are *not* leaving them behind."

Grant eased to the floor. Faith trotted up and twisted around three times before settling beside him on the edge of the living room rug. He ran a hand through her fur. Leah was right, but Grant didn't like it.

"That means we either pare it down to the minimum so we can carry it, or we have to find a car."

Leah nodded. "I vote for assembling everything we want and once everyone else shows up, we can make a decision."

"Fair enough." Grant set to work organizing the items within reach.

Everything from the kitchen went into one empty duffle bag: a can opener, collapsible bowls, their camping sporks and nesting pots. From their camping gear, he added their portable stove and fuel, all the various types of fire starters and every lighter he could find. Then knives and plastic bags and water bottles.

The bag filled faster than he expected and he hadn't even touched the food. Thanks to his haul at the sporting goods store, Grant had days' worth of freeze-dried meals. He nestled them all into a second bag along with the meager supplies left in the house and the jerky he'd picked up for Faith.

Another bag down, not nearly enough to go. Leah was right: they needed everything.

He sighed in frustration. Whenever they camped, he'd been an ultralight sort of guy. Small tent, tiny stove, pared down clothes and food. But he'd always had a home to come back to. When faced with leaving and never coming back, Grant wanted to take it all.

"Harder than it looks, isn't it?"

Grant nodded.

Leah set down the shirt she was folding. "Maybe we should stay. We could take a stand against Greg and those men."

"And then what? Wait until someone else comes along to take it all from us again?"

"The National Guard might mobilize. They might bring aid and restore the power."

Grant shook his head. "I saw downtown. There's nothing left of the state government. And if what Oliver found is true, the federal government is worse. The best we could hope for would be international aid workers."

Leah almost laughed out loud. "Never thought I'd hear you say something like that."

Grant glanced at their wall full of wedding photos. "Will and Greg are only the beginning. We have to leave."

Leah didn't say any more.

He knew she struggled with leaving everything and everyone behind. He thought about Leah's sister and finally asked the question he'd tried to avoid. "Do you want to go to Hampton?"

His wife looked away.

"We could make a life there, you and I. It would mean—"

"It would mean trading Greg for whoever is in charge there." Leah turned to face him. "How is that any better?"

"Your sister is there."

"My sister kicked you out. Her husband almost got me killed. She—" A sob cut off Leah's words and Grant crawled across the field of supplies to wrap his wife up in a hug.

"I shouldn't have brought it up."

Leah wiped her face on his shoulder. "No. It was a fair question. But I don't want to go there. I don't know if I can ever forgive them for how they treated you."

Grant leaned back and took Leah's face in his hands. "I love you and I would never have stopped looking for you."

She smiled. "Same here."

A knock on the door startled them both. Faith rushed to the front of the house, sniffing the air.

Grant stood up and headed to the door. He groaned as he opened it. "And I thought *we* had a lot of stuff."

Dan grunted beneath the weight of two massive backpacks and a cooler. "This is only half of it. The rest is in my garage."

"What about Susie and Oliver?"

Dan set the cooler down and shrugged out of both backpacks. He grabbed his knees and sucked in a lungful of air before answering. "Still packing."

Grant pinched his lips between his fingers and

turned back to his wife. "Forget a car, we're gonna need a caravan."

An hour later, Susie and Oliver trudged through the door with the last of their belongings. All told, the five of them filled the entire living room with bags and boxes and gear of all sorts.

Dan mopped his brow with a paper towel. "There's no way we're gonna be able to take all this. We need a U-Haul, not a car."

"Like a massive truck isn't a beacon for thieves." Oliver adopted a sing-song voice. "Hey bad guys, here we are, a bunch of morons in our massive truck. We don't have anything you want inside, promise."

"I didn't say it was a good idea."

Grant thought it over. "If we can find two old SUVs or a couple of pickup trucks, we might be able to haul everything."

"With your truck torched, there probably isn't a single working vehicle besides Stan's motorcycle in the neighborhood." Oliver shook his head. "Where are we going to find two?"

Dan leaned back in the chair. "I know a place. A cheap car lot on the way to Marietta. But it's too far to walk."

Oliver threw up his hands. "Lot of good that'll do, then."

Grant disagreed. "We can take the bike."

"That means two trips at least." Leah shook her head. "It'll take too long. Who knows when Greg and those thugs of his are going to come back."

"Can we both fit on the bike?"

Grant took a good look at Dan. A few inches taller, with a belly twice Grant's size, Dan had to outweigh him by fifty pounds. He hedged. "It won't be comfortable. But if we take the box off the back, maybe for one trip."

"Then let's do it. We can ride there together. If we find a big enough vehicle, the bike can go in the back. If not, we'll leave it behind."

Grant turned to his wife. "Would you be okay here? Susie and Oliver could stay. You all could take turns keeping watch."

Leah nodded. "I can do it."

Grant glanced at his watch. *Just after five.* Sunset wouldn't be for another two hours and Greg wouldn't be stupid enough to attack in the daylight. "How far is this place?"

Dan thought it over. "About twenty minutes."

"Then we should go. The faster we get there, the faster we get back."

"Give me five minutes and I'll be ready." Dan pushed off the couch and opened his backpack. He fished out a dark sweatshirt and pants before heading to the bathroom.

Grant turned to Leah. "You're sure you'll be all right?"

She nodded. "We'll be fine. Faith will let us know if anyone's snooping around."

"And if they are?"

"I'll scare them off."

"Good." Grant leaned in and kissed her quickly on

the lips before hustling to the stairs. He rummaged through his drawers before changing into clothes similar to Dan's. By the time he returned, Dan was in the garage, wrestling with the milk crate attached to the back of the bike.

Grant helped him take it off. Dan opened the garage door and Grant wheeled the bike out into the evening light. He glanced at Dan before turning back to the bike. "It won't be comfortable."

"As long as you don't throw me off, I'll be fine."

Grant eased one leg over the seat and slid as far forward as he could go. Dan clambered on behind. His belly brushed Grant's back, his thighs were uncomfortably close, and all Grant could think of were family sitcoms that would never air again.

"Ready?"

"As I'll ever be."

Grant revved the engine to life and eased onto the road before they had a chance to change their minds.

CHAPTER TEN

LEAH

2078 Rose Valley Lane
Smyrna, Georgia
Monday, 5:30 p.m.

Leah shut the single slat she could reach in the dining room window before walking back into the living room. Susie and Oliver sat on the couch, one cushion apart, looking every bit as uneasy as she felt.

She closed her eyes and leaned against the wall. So much had happened in the last week, but it still didn't feel real. Every morning she woke up expecting the world to be back to normal and all of this to be some sort of terrible dream.

Leah reached up and felt the skin around her stitches. There was no avoiding the reality of the situation with a still-healing head wound.

She pushed off the wall and headed into the kitchen.

After scooping up three glasses, she pulled the last bottle of wine off the counter.

With a smile on her face five times bigger than her mood, she held up her spoils. "Who wants a glass of wine?"

Susie glanced at Oliver. "Do you think we should?"

"If we don't lighten it up at least a little bit around here, I'm going to lose my mind." Leah set the glasses on the coffee table and unscrewed the wine. "Remind me when we find a grocery store to look for screw-top bottles. We can open these anywhere."

Oliver waited until Leah filled up all three glasses before picking one up. "I've never been a wine drinker."

Leah picked up her glass in a toast. "Here's to trying something new. It's one of the few things still good without refrigeration."

Susie lifted her glass as well and clinked it against the others. "To new adventures and new friends."

Leah gulped down a mouthful and exhaled. *A breather.* Maybe that was all she needed. She leaned back in the overstuffed chair and days of built-up tension slid off her shoulders.

"Tell me, Oliver. What did you do for a living?"

He grimaced as he sipped a bit of the wine. "Mostly freelance web design. Some backend hosting support, too." After another gulp, he shrugged. "Guess I'll be looking for a new job."

Grant worked in the computer field, too, but he wasn't hopeless without the internet. Thanks to his prior military service and general awareness, he could adapt. But Oliver was starting from scratch.

If they didn't restore order or power soon, how would he take care of himself? She glanced at Susie. How would anyone?

"I'm afraid I'm almost as useless." As if Susie read Leah's mind, she apologized. "I worked at the local nursery."

"But that means you know what grows here and what doesn't. And I've seen your garden." Leah shook her head. "Don't sell yourself short."

Susie tucked a lock of hair behind her ear. "But I can't defend myself. The way you and Grant stood up to Greg—I could never do something like that."

"You can if you put your mind to it."

Susie frowned. "It's not that easy."

"When those men were in front of the sporting goods store, I almost got us all killed." Oliver shuddered. "I didn't think they'd actually try to hurt us."

Leah swallowed. Grant had only told her the vaguest of details about that interaction. For once, she was glad he held back.

Oliver sipped more wine before holding up the glass. "The more you drink it, the better it gets."

Everyone laughed. Leah wished it could always be this easy. No fights. No threats. Nothing except good friends and good company. But it would never be this simple. Not for a long time.

Susie scooted forward on the couch. "So after Kennesaw State, where should we go?"

Oliver glanced her way. "What do you mean?"

"To live. We can't stay at a college forever."

Leah thought about her sister and the little town of Hampton. There had to be others like it all over north Georgia. "I'm sure we can find a small town that will accept us."

"But without power, what good will they be?" Oliver flopped back on the couch. "We should head north to Canada. They have power and a functioning government. It'll be like the bombs never went off."

"Until three hundred million of our closest friends try to do the same thing. The borders have to be swarmed already."

Oliver sagged. "I suppose you're right. They've probably gone on lockdown. No more migrants. Mexico's probably done the same thing."

"Wouldn't they want to help?"

"Only until their own countries were harmed. Think about the other migrant crises all over the world. At some point, every country shuts their borders."

"Then how about Vermont or Maine?" Oliver perked back up. "They should have power. The EMP didn't reach all the way up there, right?"

Leah nodded. "That's what the reporter said on television. Parts of Florida, Maine, and Vermont were still operational."

"That's where we should go, then."

"Vermont's an awful long way. It'll be overrun before we reach it."

"Do you have any better ideas?" Oliver raked a hand

through his hair and it stuck up in all directions. "We can't just stay here!"

"Sure we can." Susie set her glass on the table. "I know how to garden. Leah can treat any injuries. Dan can hunt."

"And I can be a drain. Great."

Susie leaned toward Oliver. "I didn't mean that."

He sighed. "I know. But suddenly being bad at everything isn't easy."

Leah set her glass on the table. "How about you try and get online? Maybe we can narrow down where to go."

Oliver jumped up and pulled out his laptop, punching keys faster than Leah could follow. Five minutes later, he shut the computer with a frown. "It's no use. There's nothing."

He shoved his fingers beneath his glasses and pressed on his eyes. "If the college doesn't have the capabilities to reach the outside world, I don't know if we'll ever be able to."

"Why not?"

"The satellite companies are operating at barely sufficient capacity to even allow service. It's down most of the time as it is. The only time I've been online the past week was two in the morning with a clear sky. By now, whatever backup power was running the substations on the ground might be nonfunctional."

Susie twisted on the couch. "If the college doesn't have the means to get online, what does that mean?"

Oliver turned to her. "Without leaving the United States, we're cut off."

Her mouth fell open and she turned to Leah. "Do you really think that's possible?"

"Anything is possible." Leah leaned back in the chair. "For all we know, Georgia Power's a week away from bringing us back online and the National Guard is just around the corner with trucks full of food and water."

"You can't believe that."

Leah closed her eyes. "Not a chance."

Faith hopped up and trotted into the darkness of the front of the house. Leah leaned over to catch a glimpse.

She couldn't see the dog, but she didn't have to. The low growl emanating from the darkness got the point across. Leah glanced at her watch and her eyebrows rose in alarm. Eight o'clock already? Where were Grant and Dan?

Faith growled again.

Leah eased up off the chair and motioned for Oliver and Susie to stay quiet before approaching the front door.

CHAPTER ELEVEN

GRANT

Westfield Parkway
Smyrna, Georgia
Monday 6:30 p.m.

Grant eased the motorcycle to a stop a hundred yards past the entrance to the used car lot. He killed the engine and Dan almost fell off the seat.

The older man groaned. "Thank God I'm too old for kids because after that ride, I'd never have any." He hopped around on the sidewalk, tugging down his pants.

Grant chuckled and turned to the lot. The fencing stretched all the way down the road with no gaps. "I wouldn't get too excited. Place looks pretty secure to me."

"No way. We're getting a car. Whatever it takes." Dan smoothed his hair back and cracked his neck. "How do you want to do this?"

"As easily as possible." Grant reached for his Shield

and confirmed it sat snug in his holster. "And this time, no shooting until we agree."

Dan smirked. "That'll be easy. You're the only one packing. Especially now that my balls are numb." He turned toward the car lot. "Let's go."

Grant followed Dan toward the lot. It sat in a transitional area, one of the first businesses after a stretch of overgrown forest and kudzu vines. A mile down the road, traditional car dealerships took over, offering new and used cars of every make and model.

But this lot wasn't for the ordinary consumer. With prices in big orange stickers in the low thousands, it was a place for people who could only pay cash, no questions asked.

If the owner of the lot had more sense, he'd be open with sky-high mark-ups or trades. People would pay dearly for a car that still ran.

But how many people even knew it was possible? Grant only figured it out thanks to an ancient taxi in Charlotte.

He crouched next to Dan at the fence line. "I'll do a perimeter run. Holler if you see anyone."

Dan nodded and Grant took off at a slow lope, checking the lot for any sign of activity. From the dust coating the windshields, it looked like the place had been abandoned the moment the EMP killed the power. It was deserted.

He hustled back to Dan. "It's clear." He wiped the sweat already beading on his forehead. "We need something old. No digital components."

"A POS, then."

"You could call it a classic, but yeah."

Dan eased forward and tested the fence. It didn't budge. He glanced up at the top. "Feel like climbing?"

Grant scuttled down the fence line, checking the black aluminum for gaps. He came back with a frown. At nine or ten feet tall, with nothing but aluminum posts and a top rail, it posed an impressive obstacle. Scaling it wouldn't be easy, but it was the only option.

"Looks like I don't have a choice." He stood up. "Give me a lift, will you?"

Dan interlaced his fingers and took a knee. Grant placed his foot in Dan's grip and the older man hoisted him up into the air with a wobbly grunt. Grant lunged for the fence, clawing for purchase at the top rail.

Two fingers on his left hand cleared the lip and Grant swung to the right. His right hand cleared the top and he gripped on for dear life, struggling to pull himself up. After a few agonizing moments, his chest bumped against the top. He practically flopped over, more fish out of water than graceful mountain climber, but he succeeded.

His feet landed hard on the asphalt and all the air whooshed from his lungs.

"About time. For a minute there, I thought you weren't coming back down."

Grant sucked in some air. "You could have given me a bit more of a push."

"What would be the fun in that?" Dan stood up and stretched his back. "Now find a way to let me in."

Turning toward the gate mechanism, Grant looked for any means of manual override. He popped the top and squinted into the dark interior. "Toss me that flashlight, will you?"

Dan handed a small light through the fence and Grant clicked it on. Beneath a section of gears, he found a red pull tab. *Bingo.* Grant yanked and the fence disengaged. With Dan helping from the other side, they pushed the gate open wide enough for a car.

"Looks like the SUVs are back on the far fence." Grant clicked off the light and took off through the lot with Dan right behind.

Ten boxy behemoths sat against the fence, back ends grazing the aluminum. Grant searched the row. None were old enough. Not by a long shot.

He cursed. "We need something huge to haul all the gear."

Dan ambled back toward the rear of the lot, behind the financing trailer. A gaggle of low riders with spoke rims took up the spaces. "This is what we need. A couple of these babies." He reached the first one, a dusty brown Cadillac that stretched on for miles.

"It won't traverse a river, but it'll hold the gear."

"It's a sedan."

Dan grinned. "With a six-body trunk, at least." He reached for the handle and the door swung wide open.

The interior reeked of smoke.

Grant coughed. "Hasn't been to the detail shop, I guess."

"For four hundred bucks, what do you expect?" Dan

reached in and pulled out the for sale sign before sliding into the driver's seat. He flipped the visor down searching for keys, but came up empty. "You find another car and I'll find the keys."

Grant eased around the boat on wheels and approached an Oldsmobile about a decade newer and four feet shorter. It wasn't that different from the Cutlass he drove from Charlotte to Atlanta.

Lifting his head, he searched for Dan. With no sign of him, Grant didn't wait. If it were anything like the other car, he could hotwire it before Dan found the keys. He opened the driver's door and pushed the seat all the way back.

The steering column appeared about the same, but with more plastic housing. He worked the cover back and forth until it gave before fishing out the wires. The difference in models made a difference in wires, too.

Grant frowned. He didn't know which ones to pull apart.

"Quit dicking around with the steering column and pick the keys." Grant sat up to find Dan standing in front of him with a key board in his hand. He fingered through them for an Oldsmobile tag.

The key fit in the ignition and Grant cranked it. The car sputtered. "These things are junk. We'll be lucky if we make it home."

"We'll be lucky if we ever find another working car. Try it again."

Grant cranked the key again and pumped, but the engine refused to turn over. "It's no use. This one's dead."

"Then we have to find another—"

A screech from the entry to the lot cut Dan's words short. Grant slid out of the Oldsmobile and crouched on the ground. "What was that?"

Dan lowered his bulky frame. "No idea, but it can't be good."

"Do you have the keys to the Caddy?"

"In my sweaty palm."

"See if it starts. If we can only get one car, so be it." Grant eased toward the front of the car.

"What about you?"

"I'm going to scope it out." Grant ducked around the side of the car and low-ran to the edge of the trailer. Thanks to the time it took to open the gate and then fumbling through the cars, the sun had long since passed the horizon.

Darkness set in so fast, Grant's eyes hadn't fully adjusted. He could barely see more than ten feet. *Damn it.* He pulled his gun from the holster and eased forward around the corner of the trailer.

Nothing moved.

He scurried across the open space to the first row of halfway decent sedans and ducked behind a Kia. The fence line sat twenty feet away and even though he couldn't make out more than ghostly blobs near the cars, the fence stood out against the pale concrete behind it.

The gate was shut.

Grant's stomach settled in his throat. They weren't alone in the car lot anymore.

CHAPTER TWELVE

LEAH

2078 Rose Valley Lane
 Smyrna, Georgia
 Monday, 6:30 p.m.

Leah peered through the peephole. Greg's face loomed, wide and out of proportion on the other side of the door. *Oh, no.* Leah turned and pressed her back against the wood. Nothing good could come of Greg paying them a visit.

She turned and looked again. At least three men poked around the burned-out wreckage of the truck. From the distance, Leah couldn't tell who they were, but she guessed it was the posse Greg assembled at the community meeting.

Not good. Faith ran in a circle around her legs and let out another growl. Leah wished the dog was ten times her size and rabid. Then she could take care of the men outside and Leah wouldn't have to make tough choices.

But Faith couldn't do much more than make noise. Maybe trip them up with some fancy bobbing and weaving. Leah snorted.

"Come on, Grant. I know you're in there. Open the door."

Leah didn't say a word. If she stayed quiet, Greg might go away.

Faith paced back and forth in front of Leah's feet, sniffing and grumbling.

"If you don't come out, we'll have no choice but to break down the door. I don't think you want that to happen."

Leah closed her eyes and wished for a miracle. *Please, go away.*

After a minute, Greg whammed on the door and Leah jumped. "I know you're in there. I can hear the damn dog."

Leah spun around and squinted through the peephole. Four men assembled behind Greg with some sort of log or hunk of metal. She couldn't let them break the door in. She sucked in a breath. "It's getting dark. Not the best time for a social call."

Greg grinned at his buddies. "This isn't a friendly visit. It's inventory time. Open up so we can inspect."

Crap.

No way could she open the door without Grant home. "How about we do it in the morning when there's enough light? It's super dark in here. You'll be wasting your time."

A beam of light blinded Leah through the peephole and she jerked back.

"Don't need the sun. We've got plenty of flashlights. Open up."

"Grant's sleeping. I don't want to wake him up."

Greg chuckled and his belly jiggled. "All the better. Let the man sleep and we'll be out of there before you know it."

With all of my gear and weapons. Leah frowned. She couldn't open the door. If she did that, it would all be over. Five guys, all with football builds and thick hands, would be no match for her, Oliver, and Susie.

She stared at the collection of guns on the dining room table. The air rifle, two full-size rifles, and a shotgun. It had been years since she fired a shotgun and she'd only done it a handful of times when Grant took her to an outdoor range north of town to shoot clay pigeons.

It had been fun, shooting the little clay discs out of the sky and watching them explode. But shooting a man was a heck of a lot different.

She glanced at the window. Grant had left an opening big enough to peer out of and wedge a rifle barrel in between. Could she shoot one of Dan's rifles? Would the bullet go through the window glass?

Leah had no idea, but if he didn't leave, she didn't have much of a choice. Once Greg made it inside, her ability to defend the place dropped to zero. She had to keep him out any way she could.

"What's taking so long, Leah? I don't have all night."

"I need time to get everything ready and wake Grant up. It'll be easier if we get all our things and put them in one place."

"Right. So you have time to set up an ambush? No thanks."

"It's not an ambush."

"Why should I believe you?"

"Because I don't want to hurt anyone. Not now, not ever. I'm a nurse for goodness' sake." Leah glanced down at Faith. "And I don't want you snooping around in my bedroom."

Greg laughed and Leah crossed her fingers. After a few moments, he gave in. "All right. Thirty minutes. But that's it. When we come back, I expect you to welcome us with open arms."

Leah exhaled in relief and squished her face up against the door to watch as Greg and his friends sauntered down the driveway and into the street. They were actually leaving.

She rushed back to the living room.

"What's going on?"

"Greg is demanding an inventory. He wants to come in and take all our stuff."

Susie almost leapt off the couch. "But Grant and Dan aren't home!"

"I know." Leah glanced at her watch. "They should be back soon. I stalled and got us half an hour."

"Will that be enough?"

Leah covered her collarbone with her hand. "We need to prepare for the worst. If Grant and Dan don't make it back, we'll have to defend this place."

"I've never shot a gun." Susie stared past Leah to the dining room where all their weapons sat waiting.

Oliver shoved his laptop in his messenger bag. "I don't think I can. When we were out there on the road—" He cut off in midsentence as the color fled his face.

"Maybe we could negotiate." Susie's leg bounced up and down as she talked. "We could shove part of the gear outside as a peace offering and hope they go away."

It wasn't a bad idea in theory, but Leah shook her head. "Greg will know we have more. He won't be satisfied until he takes it all."

Susie slumped in her seat. "Then we should hand it all over."

"What?" Oliver twisted to face Susie. "We can't. If they take all my equipment, we'll never get back online. How will we know where to go?"

"You said yourself, none of it works anyway. What does it matter?"

Leah held up a hand to cut the argument off. "Oliver's right. We can't hand anything over." She glanced at the front door. "Give me a minute."

She stalked back to the dining room and picked up one of Dan's rifles. Three times as heavy as the air rifle, her arm sagged with the weight. Leah pressed it against her shoulder snug and tight.

Grant had shown her how to work the lever action

earlier in the day and she knew it was loaded and ready. Dan didn't have much ammo, but with eight rounds of 30-30, she should be able to defend the house. She focused on the window.

The thought of shooting Greg made her skin crawl. Ever since the bombs, Leah survived by running and hiding. She never had to defend what was hers. It was easier to escape than stand her ground, but this time, she couldn't run.

She looked back into the house where Oliver and Susie sat in the living room, surrounded by gear. They couldn't make it out without Greg finding them and they couldn't carry all the gear. It was an impossible task.

If they were going to protect what they had, she would have to fight. Leah turned back around to the door and grabbed the door jam Grant had fashioned out of wood. She shoved it under the handle and wedged it in tight with her foot.

A battering ram would break the door down no matter what, but the jam might buy a few minutes. She picked up the other rifles and the shotgun and hurried back to Susie and Oliver. "Time for a crash course in shooting. I'm terrible at this, but try to follow."

She showed them both how to work the lever on the other rifle and where to load the ammo. Then she pumped the air rifle and explained the difference.

Oliver and Susie followed along, each asking questions Leah couldn't answer. As she finished, Susie pointed to the shotgun. "What about that one?"

Leah hesitated. "Honestly, if it comes to the shotgun,

we're probably out of luck. I don't have any idea how to load it." She picked up. "But shooting shouldn't be any different."

"Maybe Greg won't come back."

"We could still sneak out the back. Then if he breaks in, we won't be here."

Leah opened her mouth to argue when a pounding once again echoed through the house.

"Time's up! Let us in or we'll kick the door down."

"Guess we're out of options." Oliver pushed his glasses up his nose and picked up the rifle. He glanced at Susie. "We'll do our best, right?"

She nodded and Leah hurried back to the front door. After opening the slat in the shutter, she fit the rifle barrel through the plywood and let out a breath. "We changed our minds. You can't come in."

Greg laughed and Leah leaned down to line up the sights. In the dark, it was hard to make out the shapes. Was that a body or the tree in the front yard? *Crap*.

"Don't play games, Walton. Open the damn door."

"No. And if you don't go away, you'll regret it."

Greg laughed even harder and Leah's pulse quickened. He wasn't going to leave. She would actually have to do this.

His lumbering shape turned around in the driveway and other bodies separated in the dusk. *Now's my chance.*

Leah inhaled and let the air out in a slow stream to calm her jumpy hands. She focused on the shape she thought was Greg in the driveway. *All I have to do is pull the trigger.*

Her finger twitched against the metal.

I can do this.

She waited for Greg to turn around. No matter what he planned to do, Leah couldn't shoot him in the back.

As Greg began to turn, he froze. "What the hell is that?"

Leah rose up as a rumble of an engine came from the direction of the neighborhood entrance. *Grant! He's coming home!*

She smiled in relief until an air horn blasted out three times. Greg and his friends walked down toward the road, heads all pointed toward the entrance.

A strip of KC lights on a pickup truck came into view and slowed outside Leah's house. She couldn't see anything beyond the lights, but she could hear whooping and hollering and a host of shouts.

Greg and his buddies stopped moving as a megaphone clicked on.

"Attention! This is your friendly neighborhood band of thieves."

Leah swallowed.

"We're here for all your shit. So pony up, bitches!" Laughter bounced off the houses and Leah lowered the rifle.

She looked down at Faith beside her feet. "Looks like we've got bigger problems, now."

CHAPTER THIRTEEN

GRANT

Westfield Parkway
  Smyrna, Georgia
  Monday 8:00 p.m.

Grant strained to listen over the sound of his own heart. The chances of the gate shutting on its own were slim. The car lot sat flat and level, with no natural slope to guide the metal back on the track.

No, the only way the gate shut was due to a person. Someone most likely still inside. Grant worked closer to the gate, crouch-walking along the side of a car until he reached the front fender.

In the silence of the night, he could hear crickets and the steady hum of a million flying insects, all buzzing in the humid air.

There! A footstep? A scrape against a car?

Grant didn't have a clue, but he couldn't waste any

more time. If Greg decided tonight would make a good night for an ambush, Leah couldn't defend the house on her own. Susie and Oliver couldn't do much more than scream and hide in the bathroom.

I shouldn't have left them. Grant cursed at his foolishness. Now he was stuck miles from home in a car lot with someone who either wanted to flush him out, steal, or both.

He held his gun low and pointed to the ground and tensed to spring forward when someone spoke.

"Yo, D, I don't think any a' these are gonna start."

"Shut up, you idiot. Someone might hear us."

Grant eased around the front of the car and double-timed it to the end of the row.

"One of 'em's gotta work. They can't all be dead."

"Let's get to the office and find the keys. We can go one by one."

The voices were loud enough for Grant to make out all the words. Ten feet away, he guessed.

Based on the tone, Grant pegged them for a pair of teenagers looking for a new set of wheels. Maybe harmless, maybe not. But if he could find Dan and get out of there before they made it back to the working cars, he had a chance to avoid anything nasty.

Grant backpedaled down the row of cars until the trailer came into view. He turned and ran behind it, stopping once he was hidden by the building to search for Dan.

It didn't take long. The man sat behind the wheel of a beater with the dome light on with a scowl on his face.

Grant shook his head. That motorcycle might fall apart if they both had to ride it home.

"No luck?"

Dan jerked and hit his head on the visor. "Damn it. You want me to piss my pants?"

Grant grinned. "That's one way to get you off the back of the motorcycle." He motioned at the car. "No luck?"

"It's the fifth one I've tried. Can't get a single one to start."

Grant stuck his hand out. "Give me some keys. I'll see if I can find one before the kids at the front of the lot figure out we're back here."

"That's what the noise was?"

Grant nodded. "A couple of teenagers trying to boost a truck. They haven't figured out that it's hopeless."

Dan handed over a handful of keys. "Let's get this done and get out of here. I don't want any trouble."

"Neither do I." Grant clicked on the flashlight to scope out the keys. One Cadillac, an Oldsmobile, and two Buicks. He hustled up to the first Buick and tugged open the door.

A cockroach scuttled out into the night. Grant grimaced and slid into the driver's seat. He stuck the first key in the ignition. It wouldn't turn.

He tried the second. It turned and the car groaned. *Come on.* He pumped the gas and tried again, holding the key all the way forward. The engine sputtered and protested, but at last, it revved to life. *Yes!*

Grant left the engine running and ran back to Dan.

The man was now behind the wheel of a Chevy, rooting through a pile of keys.

"I got the Buick to start."

Dan shoved a key in the ignition, but it wouldn't turn. "I suppose you want a medal."

"No, but we should get out of here. Those kids will be here any second."

"You said they were harmless."

"No. I said they weren't out to get us. Not the same thing."

"Hey!"

Grant stood up. The boys from the other side of the lot stood on the stoop of the financial building. A flashlight beam hit Grant in the face.

"Yeah?"

"How'd you get that car to start?"

"Luck. Been trying them all."

"You shouldn't be helping them." Dan stuck another key in the ignition. It didn't budge.

"Why not?"

"Because they want what we have." Dan tried a third key and it cranked, but the engine didn't even wheeze. "Damn it." He thumped on the steering wheel as the flashlight beam bobbed and weaved their way.

"Get back to the car. We don't want them to steal it."

Grant sighed, but Dan had a point. He ran over the open door and fell into the driver's seat just as one of the kids reached the front of the car. With a yank of the handle, Grant slammed the door shut.

The kids' hands slapped the driver's window.

Knobby knuckles. Palms creased with dirt. He bent down and grabbed the handle.

Grant pushed the lock down and glared. "I wouldn't do that if I were you."

"Yeah? Well, you're not me. Out of the car, old man."

"Not a chance." Grant brought the Shield up into view. "Back up or I'll put a hole right through this window and your chest."

The kid raised his arms and Grant used his free hand to click on the flashlight. He shone it right in the kid's face.

With a scraggly, barely-there beard and wide brown eyes, he couldn't have been older than seventeen. Grant frowned. "If you'd asked for help, I'd have been more than willing."

"Right. And I got a wad of cash in my back pocket and a girlfriend waiting for me back home."

"Where's your friend?" Grant peered around the kid, using the flashlight to get a better look. Dan wasn't sitting inside the Chevy.

Grant spun around, lighting up all the cars within his immediate area. No sign of Dan or another kid. He turned back to the one at the window.

He was gone.

Shit.

Grant killed the engine and pocketed the keys. He couldn't leave with Dan out there somewhere, but he couldn't risk the kids driving off in their only working car. He shut the door and used the flashlight to search. With his night vision destroyed, he couldn't look for Dan any other way.

If the other kid had a gun, he'd be in a world of hurt, but Grant didn't think either one was armed. He cupped one hand around his mouth. "Dan! Where are you?"

A muffled shout echoed across the lot and Grant took off. The flashlight beam bounced as his feet hit the pavement and Grant shouted again. "Dan!"

This time the older man managed to get his mouth free. "Pissant's got a .22 up against my ribs."

Hell.

Grant clicked off his light and squeezed his eyes shut. After counting to ten, he opened them. The darkness eased into blobs and shapes. It would have to do.

Hurrying toward the last place he heard Dan's voice, Grant kept his feet light and his noise to a minimum. It didn't take long to find them.

The bright burning end of a cigarette led Grant to within five feet of the teenagers. One held Dan by the arms with his forearms locked up underneath Dan's shoulder blades. Dan's gut stuck out in front of him like a beached whale and from the pained expression on his face, he hated every second of it.

The other kid held a snubnosed revolver in one hand and a cigarette in the other. He sucked down a lungful of nicotine before blowing a cloud of smoke into Dan's face.

"You blow that crap in my face one more time and it'll be your face that's on fire next."

The kid laughed before shoving the cigarette

between his lips. He coiled back to punch Dan in the gut when Grant stepped forward.

"Don't even think about it." The kid spun around and Grant took aim. "If you so much as look at him again, I'll shoot."

The kid waggled the little revolver in the air and spoke out of the free side of his mouth. "Don't you see what I'm holdin'? You shoot me and I shoot you."

"Ever shot a teensy little gun like that before? They can't aim for shit."

"Oh and yours can?"

"Better than that toy you're holding."

The kid glanced down at the gun and Grant took a chance. He aimed at the kid's upper leg and fired. A scream cut through the night air and the kid's gun flew from his hand and clattered on the pavement

"You shot me! You freakin' shot me!"

Grant didn't bother to reply, ignoring the kids wails and shouts as he hopped around on one foot. He focused on the other kid still holding Dan. "Let him go or you'll have a matching bullet wound."

Dan grunted. "Shoot him. They can be twins."

The kid let Dan go. The older man spun around and decked him square in the jaw and he stumbled back, hitting the hood of a sedan before crumpling to the ground.

Dan shook out his hand. "Frisk him, will you? He's got the keys to a Dodge that runs."

Grant bent down and rifled through the kid's pockets

until he found a set of keys. He motioned toward the back lot. "Let's get the hell out of here."

"What about the bike?"

"Leave it. If they can figure out how to ride it, they can have it." Grant tossed the motorcycle key on the ground. "There's a bike in the bushes outside the gate. Good luck getting your buddy on the back."

Grant rushed over to the gate and pushed it open before following Dan's form through the lot. The kid with the bullet wound shouted obscenities at their backs.

Dan tugged open the door to a two-door Dodge, three cars down from the Buick. "Meet you at your place?"

"Sounds good to me." Grant slid behind the wheel of the Buick and fired it up while Dan cranked the Dodge. He waited for Dan to back out before following him out through the front of the lot and onto the road.

The kids had managed to hobble over to the bike and the one with two working legs straddled the seat. Grant shook his head. The poor guy didn't stand a chance.

As the Buick coasted out of the lot and onto the road, Grant found the headlights and flicked them on. He couldn't wait to get back to his wife.

CHAPTER FOURTEEN

LEAH

2078 Rose Valley Lane
Smyrna, Georgia
Monday, 8:00 p.m.

"What's going on?" Susie braved the front of the house with Leah's air rifle gripped tight in her hands.

"We have company and they're way less polite than Greg."

Susie's eyes went wide as Leah ushered her up to look through the slat in the window. From their vantage point, the women could make out the two houses across the street, the truck stopped with the row of overhead lights blazing on top, and a gaggle of men lit up like stage actors on a play in front.

"Who are they?"

"No idea, but they have a megaphone and they want our stuff."

Susie pulled back in alarm. "How do they know we have anything?"

Leah shrugged. "It's a nice neighborhood. I'm assuming they think we're better off than most."

"What are we going to do?"

"Watch and see what happens. Maybe Greg will talk some sense into them."

Susie almost choked. "I don't think that man knows what common sense is."

Leah turned back to the window. Men from the truck hopped down and entered the light. They all wore masks. Not balaclavas or ski masks, or even pantyhose over their faces like criminals in half the thrillers Grant loved to watch.

No, little kid Halloween masks. There was a dog, a frog, and—Leah squinted to make it out—a fairy? She shook her head. Their masks distracted from what really mattered: the crowbars and baseball bats in their hands.

One man separated himself from the rest of the pack and approached Greg, who stood on the edge of the pool of light. Thick dreads sprouted from the top of the man's head and stuck up above his unicorn mask, making him look like a half horse, half lion.

He held a megaphone out to the side and one of his compatriots plucked it from his hand. Leah pressed her lips together. Without the megaphone she wouldn't be able to hear.

She spun around. The guest bedroom upstairs fronted the street. She reached for Susie. "Stay here and keep watch. I'm going to listen from upstairs."

Leah raced up to the second floor and Faith followed right on her heels. The tree in their front yard hid most of the second floor from view, but she could still make out the men in the street through the branches.

Leah set the rifle on the floor and unlocked the window. The metal thwacked into place and she froze. If they heard her, would they come for their house first? For all she knew Greg was selling her out right now, claiming she had all the gear in here and if they only busted into her house, they could leave everyone else alone.

She had to hear what they were saying, even if it meant exposing her location. With a tight grip on both pulls, Leah lifted the window. Humid night air rushed into the room, carrying the voices from the street.

"—don't understand. We ain't here for no social visit. Get outta my way."

Greg crossed his arms and widened his stance. The KC lights from the truck shone right in his face. "This isn't some store you can ransack for TVs and new sneakers. Go find the Walmart down the road. It's got everything you could need."

The man opposite him turned to the frog mask wearer and laughed. "You hear that? This fool thinks I want a TV." He turned back around. "I don't want your fancy flat screen TVs. I want your guns."

Leah shivered.

"You really think any of the people in this neighborhood are going to give you their weapons?"

"Damn straight, I do."

Greg shook his head in disbelief. "Then you're even

crazier than that mask makes you look. You knock on the wrong door and someone will shoot you on the front step."

Leah hated to agree with anything that came out of Greg's mouth, but the man was right. If anyone tried to steal the rifle at Leah's feet, she would shoot first and worry about the consequences later.

Mr. Unicorn reached behind him and pulled something out of his waistband. Leah's heart dove for her stomach as the man pointed a handgun at Greg's chest.

The interlopers weren't without guns. They wanted more.

Greg's hands rose into the air. "I'm not armed."

"Too bad for you." Mr. Unicorn held out his free hand. The frog handed the megaphone back. "Attention, all you greedy, selfish bastards in this 'hood. We are here for your weapons. You have a gun? Bring it out. You got a metal baseball bat? That bitch is mine. Switchblade? Come to daddy. All of it."

He took a step closer to Greg. "Or this asshole standing out here like he's king gets popped."

Leah swallowed. They wouldn't kill him, would they? Greg might be a jerk with a superiority complex, but he had kids and a wife and worked at Home Depot. He wasn't the head of some rival gang or some mastermind criminal.

Not that these guys were, either. Of all the people in the neighborhood to hold as ransom, Greg was the worst choice. Leah chewed on her lip. From where she crouched, Grant could take out the guy with the gun.

But Leah hadn't ever fired a full-sized rifle. She picked up the gun and brought it to her shoulder to aim. The barrel wobbled in the air. She was just as likely to shoot Greg as Mr. Unicorn or miss entirely and take out someone else.

And if she missed, everyone would know what house to attack first.

Leah lowered the gun. Whatever happened to Greg out there, he was on his own.

The man in the unicorn mask chortled orders to each of his guys and they fanned out across the street, rushing up to front doors and pounding. He clicked on the megaphone again. "Let me repeat myself. If you have any weapons, bring them outside. Now."

He stuck the handgun straight up toward the sky and pulled the trigger. The shot echoed through the neighborhood like a massive clap of thunder. "Next time, I aim straight for this chump's face."

The door to Greg's house flew open and Jennifer tore down the street in a bathrobe and bare feet. "Stop! That's my husband."

Greg moved toward her, but Mr. Unicorn pointed the gun back at his chest.

Jennifer rushed up to stand between them. "You don't have any reason to shoot him. He wasn't doing anything."

"Jennifer. What are you doing? Go back inside."

She shook her head, but didn't turn around. "No. I'm not letting you get shot out here." She turned back to the man in the mask. "If you let my husband go, I'll tell you what houses have weapons."

Leah's mouth fell open. It didn't take a genius to know which house she would point out first.

"Jen, no! Don't do it."

She finally turned to face Greg. "Why not? What do we care if some of the people around here lose their advantage? You were going to do the same thing."

Greg looked like he was about to throw up. He ran a hand through his hair and looked around. "This isn't right. You should go back inside."

"No. I'm not letting you die out here."

The thief waggled the gun at Greg. "You really gonna let your old lady do the heavy lifting?"

Greg turned to look at Leah's house. She didn't know if he was detailing ratting them out or wishing they would come to his rescue, but it didn't matter. Either way, he'd probably be shot in the end. These guys didn't seem like the sort to leave loose ends.

He turned back to Mr. Unicorn. "You let my wife go back inside and I'll tell you all I know. There aren't a ton of guns in the neighborhood, but I know a few houses that have what you want."

The unicorn mask bobbed up and down. "That's more like it." He waved at Jennifer. "Get her out of here."

"What? No! Honey, what are you doing?"

He smiled at his wife. "The right thing. Go inside."

Two men reached under her arms and hauled her back toward her house. She fought them every step of the way. "You're going to get yourself killed!" She pointed up at Leah's house. "Just tell them about Grant!"

Leah's breath caught in her throat. The unicorn mask tipped to the side. "Who's Grant?"

Greg didn't answer right away.

Mr. Unicorn stepped closer and pointed the gun at Greg's forehead. "Who the hell is Grant?"

"He's a neighbor."

Leah blinked. So far Greg hadn't sold them out, but that could change any moment. She picked up the rifle and brought it into position.

"What neighbor?"

Greg paused again. Leah brought one leg up to a ninety-degree angle and rested her elbow on her thigh. Now was her chance to shoot the mask-wearing man and end this. If Greg ratted them out, she'd have a bigger problem. If he didn't, then she'd owe him.

Either way, she needed to make the tough choice. Leah sucked in a breath and let it out, slow and steady. Her finger found the trigger and she jammed the butt of the rifle as tight to her shoulder as it would go. Lowering her head down into position, she sighted on the man's chest.

Everything slowed. Time. Movement. Energy.

I can do this. It's like shooting a clay pigeon, just with blood and death attached.

She tensed to squeeze the trigger when Greg lunged. His whole body came forward as Leah fired.

Time sped up to warp speed.

Greg yanked Mr. Unicorn off center with his hand

around the barrel of the handgun. The round discharged from Leah's gun, and she jerked back from the recoil. Mr. Unicorn fired his own weapon as he stumbled forward.

She fell back and shouts erupted.

Leah scrambled toward the window as the simultaneous gunshots echoed against the dark houses. Both Mr. Unicorn and Greg had fallen to the ground.

Did I get him? She waited with lungs full of pent-up air. Mr. Unicorn staggered to his feet, gun still in his hand. Blood coated his chest and his left arm.

Greg didn't get up.

Leah exhaled.

Jennifer screamed. The two men holding her let her go and she rushed up to Greg's body on the ground, bathrobe flying open to reveal a chemise and nothing more. She fell to her knees in the middle of the street.

"No!" Blood wicked up her robe as she tried to lift Greg's lifeless body. "No!"

She spun on the shooter. "How could you! He was going to tell you what you wanted!"

Mr. Unicorn staggered in the street. He transferred the gun to his left hand before grabbing his left bicep. Blood oozed between his fingers.

Leah swallowed. Her shot was accurate. If Greg hadn't lunged, she would have hit her target square on. Instead, she tagged his arm. Assuming he stopped the bleeding, the man wouldn't die.

Damn it.

The man ripped off his mask and looked around

before stalking up to Jennifer. He yanked her onto her feet by her hair.

She screamed even louder.

He jabbed the gun into her temple, grinding the barrel into her skin. "Someone shot me. Who was it?"

CHAPTER FIFTEEN

GRANT

Rose Valley Lane
Smyrna, Georgia
Monday, 9:00 p.m.

The car bottomed out as Grant turned toward his subdivision. With close-to-flat tires and a shot suspension, the Buick was years past its prime. But as long as it fit people and gear and got them on the road, it would have to do. At some point, they could find something better.

He slowed to turn into his neighborhood when two pops made him stop. Were those gunshots? Pulling over to the side of the road, he flashed his lights for Dan to slow.

The other man stopped and backed up his car until it sat parallel to Grant. Dan cranked the window down. "What's the matter?"

"Gunshots. Two of them, from somewhere inside the neighborhood."

"Are you sure?"

Grant rubbed his chin. "No. But there would have been more if it had been firecrackers."

As they sat idling a hundred feet from the turn-in, shouts flitted through the silent houses. Grant strained to listen, but he couldn't make out the words.

"Something isn't right. I say we stash the cars and go in on foot. If Greg is up to no good, the last thing we need is him wrecking another vehicle."

Dan grumbled, but agreed. "We can pull into the warehouse just down the road. The parking lot has some stalled cars in it. These will blend in."

"Perfect." Grant waited for Dan to pull out before joining him back on the road. He turned off his headlights and crawled past the entrance to the neighborhood.

He didn't like what he saw.

A quarter of a mile past the entrance, Grant pulled into the parking lot and eased the car in between a Camry and a Rav-4 and killed the engine. He pocketed the keys and met Dan in the lot. "There's a truck in the road on Rose Valley with a light bar all lit up. I don't recognize it."

"See any people?"

"A ton. All in the road near my house."

Dan cursed. "We can sneak down Canary and come around to Rose Valley from the back."

Grant checked both the Shield and his second

magazine. "If Greg has done anything to Leah or the others, I'm not giving him a free pass."

"Neither am I." Dan shook out his hand, now swollen from punching the kid. "After that fiasco in the car lot, I'm not in much of a nice-guy mood."

Together, they headed toward the landscaping flanking the entrance to the neighborhood. Grant eased around a clump of bushes and into the front yard of the first house on the street.

Fifteen houses ahead, the truck's lights lit up the end of Rose Valley. Grant could make out four people standing in the road and a cluster of moving bodies closer to the truck.

"Recognize it?" He motioned at the truck as Dan came up alongside him.

"Nope. You think it's someone visiting?"

"Not the friendly sort." Grant eased around the house and into the shadows before crossing another yard. Dan kept close and they reached Canary Avenue without issue. As soon as the lights from the truck faded behind the houses, Grant took off in a jog. Whatever was happening down by his house didn't look good.

The road swooped around in a giant, flat U behind Rose Valley and came back up the other side. Halfway down the street, a scream stopped Grant still.

A man's voice rang out through the space between the houses. "Someone shot me! Who was it?"

Grant rushed between the houses on Canary and scrambled over the fence to his next-door neighbor's backyard. Keeping below the top of the fence line, he hurried to the gate. Harvey never locked it.

With steady fingers, he lifted the latch and eased the wood gate open. It creaked and he froze.

A man stood in the beam of the truck's light bar, holding Greg's wife by the hair. He ground the barrel of a handgun into her temple as she sobbed. Dreads spread halfway down the man's back and in the light, Grant could make out a giant snake tattoo curving over his non-wounded arm. Blood dripped off his left hand as he twisted Jennifer's hair.

Grant swallowed.

Greg's body lay in a pool of blood in front of Jennifer. She screamed as the man yanked her harder.

"Don't make me ask again. Who shot me? Who was it?" His face contorted into a sneer and a piercing stood out in relief on his eyebrow.

Tears mixed with a smear of blood across Jennifer's cheek as she lifted a shaky hand. She pointed straight at Grant's house and his veins turned to ice. "It had to be Grant."

The man dumped Jennifer on the ground and she scrabbled over to her husband's dead body. Sobbing, she clutched at his shoulders. Greg's head lolled to the side.

Something brushed Grant's arm and he jumped. Dan stood beside him, panting and out of breath. "Next time you decide to take a shortcut, pick the old-man-friendly route."

Grant motioned to the street. "These guys are trouble. Greg's dead. Jennifer's freaking out."

"Who shot him?"

"I don't know, but she blamed me for the man with gun's arm wound."

Dan leaned close enough to get a look out the open gate. "I've never seen him before."

"What about the rest of them?"

Dan leaned closer to peer around Grant's shoulder. "Logan's over by the burned-out truck with three other guys. Must be Greg's men."

Grant counted who he could see. "So that's six strangers and four neighborhood guys." From what Grant could figure out, Greg and the man with the arm wound must have gotten into it. At least it meant the neighborhood hadn't brought in reinforcements.

But could they count on Greg's men to fight? Grant glanced up at his house. Where was Leah? Did she shoot the man or was Jennifer just using their house as an excuse?

Two of the men ran up to the one with the gun and Grant's mouth fell open. "Are they wearing masks?"

"I'm guessing they aren't here for some messed-up birthday party."

Grant clenched his fist. "We can't let them break in to my house."

"There's six of them at least and only two of us."

"Everything we own is in there."

Dan shook his head. "We're walking into a fight we can't win."

"Would you rather they break in, get all our supplies

and guns, and do who knows what to Leah, Susie, and Oliver?"

"Damn it." Dan wiped sweat off his forehead. "I should have brought a rifle."

"We should have done a lot of things." Grant held his gun pointed toward the ground. "I'll lead, you stick to the house. Keep anyone from breaking in."

"What if they've got a gun?"

Grant hesitated. "Then I guess you run like hell and hope you don't get shot."

"Great." Dan hoisted up his pants. "If I knew I'd need to be a sprinter when the end of the world came, I'd have laid off the beer."

Grant pushed the gate open wide enough to fit through and sidestepped to the edge of his house. Creeping between just-emerging hostas and lilies, he eased up to the corner.

Even rusty, he was a reliable shot at twenty yards, but he couldn't identify any of the men in the street. If they were neighbors caught up in the melee and he shot them, he would never forgive himself. *I have to get closer.*

Grant darted around the corner of the house and ducked behind the row of bushes obscuring most of the front porch. The burnt-out truck still sat in the driveway. With a deep breath, Grant took off for it, keeping close to the house as he rushed up the side of the garage and around the front corner.

"Hey!"

Grant ducked behind the front end of the truck.

"You! Get out here!"

He sucked in a breath. He hadn't made it unnoticed. Crouching low, Grant crept toward the far side of the truck.

A pair of boots stomped up the driveway on the other side. "Where the hell you at?"

Grant came even with the boots, moving down the length of the truck as the person on the other side advanced. Two men stood at the end of his driveway. One turned his way and Grant recognized him: Logan from the meeting.

He motioned to the street and mouthed, "How many?"

Logan stared at him for a moment before holding up an open hand and then one finger. *Six men.*

Grant pointed at his gun. *Any armed?*

Logan reduced his finger count to two.

Two armed men, one of them chasing him around the side of the truck. Not the best odds, but he didn't have a choice. He was already exposed.

Grant sucked in a breath and took off at a run, darting across Harvey's driveway and into the bushes in front of the old man's house.

"There he is!"

Grant backed up, keeping low enough for the bushes to cover him, but clear enough to shoot. Thanks to the truck's lights, he could see not only the street, but all of Harvey's yard. A man in a frog mask bounded up the driveway with a crowbar in his hand.

Grant lifted his Shield and took aim. He fired and hit the man square in the chest. The frog mask dipped and the man stared at his chest for a moment before sinking to his knees.

Another man in a dog mask ran up to his buddy carrying what looked to be a shotgun. Grant fired and hit him in the thigh. The man screamed and dropped the gun.

Logan and two of his friends took off running, zigzagging out of the light and into grassy front yards. Grant let them go.

Thanks to the masks, Grant could tell the groups apart.

Grant waited behind the bushes for another of the intruders to show up, but after the two fatalities, everyone scattered. The lit-up space in front of the truck stood empty apart from Greg's lifeless body. Even Jennifer had disappeared.

He chewed on the inside of his cheek as he searched the area for any sign of movement.

As he squinted at the tree across the street, the truck's lights clicked off. The neighborhood plunged into darkness. Grant couldn't see a thing.

CHAPTER SIXTEEN

LEAH

Rose Valley Lane
  Smyrna, Georgia
  Monday, 10:00 p.m.

Leah watched the gun-toting dog-face man fall to the ground and she cheered. Either someone from Greg's crew had finally decided to take a stand, or her husband made it back home.

She bet all the food in their house that it was Grant. Bending down, Leah lined up the sight and scanned the street for any attackers. No one risked getting caught in the headlights.

With two men down and one injured, that left three of the newcomers and all of Greg's men. But without Greg, Leah wasn't sure they would attack. After Mr. Unicorn killed Greg, they definitely weren't going to join forces.

She had to assume both still wanted their supplies.

As she stared out into the street, the truck lights shut off. *Crap.* She couldn't see a thing and neither could anyone else.

Leah stood up and rushed downstairs. Oliver and Susie cowered together in the kitchen, as far away from windows and doors as they could manage. Susie rose up as Leah came in.

"What's going on? There were gunshots! Screaming!"

"The neighborhood is under attack. Six men at least, all wearing masks."

"Are they shooting neighbors?"

"Greg is dead. Someone else shot two of the thieves and they're down." Leah sucked in a breath. "I shot their leader, but only in the arm. He's still mobile and madder than a hornet in a jar."

Oliver stood up, clutching the rifle. "What should we do?"

"I think Grant is out there. He's the one who shot the newcomers."

"What about Dan?"

"I haven't seen him."

Susie swallowed. "Are Greg's men still out there?"

"I don't know. Some ran away, but it's too dark. I couldn't see who."

Leah turned to head back out the front of the house when the back door rattled. She put her finger to her lips to keep Oliver and Susie quiet.

The door rattled again and the handle shook. Thanks

to the jam Grant shoved underneath the handle, Leah thought it would hold, but not forever. She brought the rifle up into position and wedged it against her shoulder.

"Hello? Is anyone in there?" The door rattled again.

Leah tilted her head. "Dan, is that you?"

"Yes. Let me in."

She stepped forward, but Susie rushed up with a warning hand. She spoke barely above a whisper. "Don't open the door."

Leah frowned. "Why not?"

"It doesn't sound like Dan. We need to make sure." Susie called out. "Are you all right?"

"No. I've been shot. I need some help. Please, let me in."

Shot? How? Leah glanced at Susie. The older woman was shaking her head no. Leah didn't know what to do. She couldn't leave Dan out there to die in her backyard, but she couldn't risk letting in a stranger, either.

She hedged. "Hold on. I've got to get the stuff off the door to open it."

The voice on the other side sounded pained. "Hurry."

Leah turned to Oliver and waved him over. "Get the flashlight and go upstairs. The guest room looks out on the backyard. If you can shine that light down by the door, you can see who it is. If it's Dan, holler and I'll let him in."

"What if it isn't?"

"Turn off the light and run like hell. If he's armed, you don't want to get shot."

Oliver nodded and grabbed the light off the couch before scurrying up the stairs.

Leah glanced at Susie. "Are you sure that isn't Dan?"

Susie nodded. "Very."

Leah bounced back and forth on the balls of her feet, waiting for Oliver. He was taking forever. After another minute, she shook her head. "Something's wrong. I'm going up there."

She hurried up the stairs. "Oliver? What's the matter? Can't you—"

The barrel of a gun emerged from the guest bedroom followed by a thick arm wrapped around Oliver's neck. "Back up."

Leah complied, retreating down the hallway as a burly man she'd never seen before shoved Oliver forward. "How did you get in here?"

"Not too hard when everyone's distracted."

She stumbled. "You mean Dan at the back door?"

The burly man mocked her. "I'm hurt, please help me."

Leah ground her teeth together. Susie had been right not to open the door and Leah was a few steps away from letting some stranger in the house. If Dan wasn't in the backyard, where was he? And where was Grant?

Her heel slipped off the landing to the stairs and Leah grabbed the rail to keep from falling. "What do you want with us?"

"Everything you have, to start. Then we can talk about what else." The man eyed her with a look that made Leah's skin crawl.

He motioned for her to go downstairs and Leah complied, easing down one stair at a time, all the while focusing on the man and Oliver. Based on his blue lips and fingers that weakly clutched at the man's arm, Oliver wasn't getting enough oxygen to stay conscious much longer.

Once he passed out, the man wouldn't have anything weighing him down. Leah had to act before that happened. She paused at the landing halfway down the stairs. "I'm not alone. You really think you can take all of us?"

The man raised a bushy eyebrow. "Like anyone around here knows what to do with a gun." He waved the pistol in his hand at Leah's rifle. "You ever even shoot that thing?"

"Enough to be dangerous."

He chuckled. "To yourself, maybe. Now get downstairs and let my buddy in."

Leah swallowed and glanced down into the first floor. She couldn't see Susie anywhere, but their giant pile of gear and food was more than obvious. As soon as the man holding Oliver hostage got a look at it, he'd probably shoot them all and be done with it.

She focused on Oliver and closed her eyes in slow motion before taking another step. *Please get the hint.* His brow wrinkled. Leah repeated the movement, closing her eyes and sagging a bit as she retreated another step.

"Something wrong with you? Why are you slumping over?" The man yanked on Oliver as he cleared the landing.

Leah was running out of time. She stared at Oliver. If he didn't help her, she would have to risk shooting him. At last, he either got the hint or the lack of oxygen took its toll. His eyelids drooped. His fingers slipped off the man's arm.

Leah backed down a quick three steps as Oliver's body sagged with unconscious weight. The man took his eyes off Leah to hoist Oliver's lifeless body up and Leah took the chance.

She jerked the rifle up into position, aimed at the man's shoulder opposite Oliver, and fired. The kickback tossed her back down the last two steps and she landed hard on her butt on the wood floor.

The burly man looked down at his shoulder, but didn't even wobble.

Did I miss?

Blood bloomed on his pale shirt and Leah blinked. She hit him right where she aimed, but he didn't act like it even hurt. What kind of a man was he? She brought the rifle back up and aimed at his head, but it was too late.

The man aimed back with his pistol. "Shoot me again and I'll make sure to have some fun with you before you die."

Leah lowered the rifle. The man tossed Oliver down the remaining steps. His body landed in a heap next to Leah. She reached out and felt for a pulse. Slow and steady. He would wake up soon.

As the man hit the floor, he grabbed Leah by the arm and yanked her up to stand. She struggled in his grip, trying in vain to get the rifle into position. He kicked at her hand holding the barrel and the rifle flew out of her grip and across the room.

Before she could scream, his arm flew back and his knuckles collided with her face. Leah's head whipped to the side. Her brain beat against her skull. She swooned.

"Get over there and open the back door." With a mighty shove, he launched Leah toward the back door.

She staggered. Her brain felt like applesauce. *I can't pass out. I have to stay awake.* She struggled toward the door, barely registering Susie in the kitchen.

The man still claiming to be Dan knocked on the door. "Please let me in. I've been shot. There's blood everywhere."

Leah stumbled as she reached for the door. The whole room spun. Nausea brought bile and spit up her throat. She gagged.

The booming blast of a gunshot behind her snapped her head back. Leah turned around and the world spun with her. The man who punched her and choked Oliver into unconsciousness lay facedown on the floor.

A massive gaping hole marred his back.

Leah tried to process. She lifted her head. Susie stood in the kitchen, holding the shotgun in both hands, frozen. Leah blinked to clear the dimming of her vision. A ringing sounded in her ears.

She staggered, searching for a chair or a table to hold onto. The world cut to black and Leah passed out.

CHAPTER SEVENTEEN

GRANT

Rose Valley Lane
Smyrna, Georgia
Monday, 10:00 p.m.

Grant blinked in vain. Without the truck's lights, he couldn't see a thing. *Shit.* He ran a hand through his hair and glanced around. He needed that truck.

Thanks to the full-size bed, it would haul most of their gear and they wouldn't have to leave much behind. They had to have it.

He sucked in a breath and took off, running straight for the truck. *I can't see, neither can anyone else.* Grant stopped at the body of the man in the dog mask and picked up the shotgun. *So far, so good.*

Racing down the driveway and into the road, he tore around the side of the truck and stumbled to a stop. A man stood beside the back end, rooting underneath a tarp.

Grant brought the shotgun up. "Stop. Put your hands where I can see them."

The man jerked back and his hands shot into the air. Even though Grant was only a handful of steps away, he couldn't make out the man's features.

"Identify yourself."

"John Peplum. I live on Wren over by Logan."

Grant frowned and stepped forward. The tattoos covering the stranger's arms reminded him of the man who held Jennifer in the street. He pointed with the gun barrel. "Do you have any identification? Something to prove it?"

"Not with me."

"If I let you go, what will you do?"

The man didn't answer. Grant leaned over and put the man's chest in his sights. He couldn't risk a lie or a double-cross.

As he exhaled, a shape emerged from the shadows behind the stranger. Grant jerked the gun that way as Dan's face came close enough for Grant to see.

"Don't go shooting me, now." Dan squinted at the other man. "John, right?'

He nodded.

"You know him?"

"He's a friend of Logan's."

Grant lowered the gun. "Are you sure?"

Dan nodded. "I saw him at the meeting."

And I was about to shoot him. Grant held the shotgun out to Dan and waited until the older man took it before motioning to John. "Get out of here unless you want to get shot for real."

The man took off without saying a word. Grant leaned against the truck. "I didn't believe him." He wiped at his face. "It's only been a few days and I was willing to shoot him on the off-chance he was lying."

Dan checked the shotgun. "Don't blame you. How many more are out there?"

Grant tallied it up in his head. "With John taking off, all of Greg's men are accounted for. I saw Logan and two others run earlier. There's two dead mask-wearers."

"I counted six, total, including the one with dreads."

"That leaves three uninjured, and their leader with a gunshot wound to the arm."

Grant nodded. "We have to take them out." He motioned at the truck. "Cover me."

While Dan stood guard, Grant clambered up into the truck. He reached for the ignition and almost whooped for joy. The keys were there. He pocketed them and hurried back to the ground. "I've got the keys. If we can find the stragglers, we can end this."

A muffled gunshot echoed in the stillness and Grant jerked up. "Was that—?"

"At your house? It sure sounded like it." Dan pointed with the shotgun. "Go and I'll cover you."

Grant took off for his house, keeping low, but not stopping until he reached the front door. He slammed a fist on the wood. "Leah! Leah!" He tried the knob. Locked.

If that gunshot was inside, then whoever broke in came through the back. Grant rushed around the side with his handgun ready. The fence gate hung loose on its hinges, splintered where he'd locked the handle.

Grant cursed. If Leah was hurt, he'd never forgive himself. *I was out there worrying about a truck and she was inside...*

He eased toward the backyard. At the edge of the house, he leaned forward just far enough to poke his head around. Thanks to the clearing of the clouds, the moonlight gave him enough light to see.

A man stood by the back door, holding a crowbar as he paced. Grant didn't waste any time. It didn't matter if he was a thief, one of Greg's buddies, or a random stranger. Leah was in trouble.

Stepping fully into the backyard, Grant aimed and fired. The first bullet hit the man in the shoulder and Grant fired again. The intruder crumpled to the ground.

Grant rushed up to the back door and tried the handle. Locked. He frowned and stepped back. It was then he saw the ladder. Harvey always left random equipment in his backyard. A ladder one week. A circular saw the next. Always tinkering, never finishing everything.

The window upstairs stood open. Grant fished his keys out of his pocket and unlocked the door. It took all his strength and three well-aimed kicks to knock it down thanks to the door jam.

Tumbling into the room, Grant tripped over something warm and soft. He landed on his knees beside his wife. "Leah!"

She lolled like a rag doll as he flipped her over. No obvious wounds. He felt for a pulse. Steady and strong.

Grant jerked his head up. A man lay on the floor, facedown in a sticky pool of blood. The gunshot.

Past him, Oliver slumped over in a heap. Grant rushed to him. Blue lips and cold fingers, but otherwise fine. His heart still beat.

What the hell happened here?

It was then he heard the whimper. Grant stood up and checked his gun. He eased back around the corner and into the kitchen. Faith stood beside Susie, whimpering and pawing the woman's leg.

Susie didn't move. She held Grant's shotgun in her hands and stared off into space like a wax figurine.

The light from the lanterns cast the whole place in an artificial glow and Grant could almost believe it was a dream. He reached for Susie. She twitched at his touch.

Her fingers stayed locked around the shotgun.

"Susie? Susie it's Grant. Can you hear me?"

He pried first one finger and then another off the stock of the shotgun, finally dislodging it from her grip. Still, she didn't acknowledge him.

"Susie? Susie are you all right?"

"Whoa."

Grant looked up.

Dan stepped over the dead man on the floor and came to a stop in the kitchen. "What the hell happened?"

Grant shook his head. "As far as I can tell, Susie saved everyone's lives."

CHAPTER EIGHTEEN

LEAH

Rose Valley Lane
   Smyrna, Georgia
   Tuesday, 1:00 a.m.

"You should try and sleep."

"I can't. What if I have a concussion but the symptoms don't present until I'm asleep?"

Grant reached out and took Leah's hand. "I can wake you up."

She glanced at the stain on the floor where the dead man oozed blood all over. "I don't think I could sleep even if I tried."

"Fair enough." Grant leaned back and wiped his eyes.

"But if you're tired, you should try. I can keep watch until the morning."

"No. I'm too keyed up to sleep."

Leah sipped the instant hot chocolate her husband made on their portable stove after everyone else went to bed. It wasn't as good as the real thing, but she didn't mind. Something hot and sweet went a long way toward putting the events of the last few hours behind her.

"You did a great job defending this place."

Leah snorted. "You mean Susie did. All I did was shoot a guy in the arm, start a turf war, forget the upstairs wasn't secure, and almost get all of us killed."

She shook her head. "I even shot the guy who broke in and he acted like it was a pin prick."

Grant glanced at the kitchen counter where all the guns rested, waiting to be cleaned. "You use the rifle?"

Leah nodded.

"Close range?"

"About five feet."

Her husband whistled. "That close and the round would be a through-and-through. I've seen guys get hit four or five times like that and keep coming. The bullet hole is too small and the round is traveling too fast to do serious damage that close."

Leah set her mug down with a clunk. "Now you tell me."

"I didn't think you'd need to fire it inside."

"So we need more shotguns and pistols?"

"Those would be a good start." Grant scrubbed his face. "More of everything. A lot more."

Leah thought about everything that happened and how brave Susie, Oliver, and Dan had been. Thanks to each of them, no one in their little group was seriously injured.

Oliver woke up not too long after she did. Apart from a bruise around his neck and a few from where he fell, he was fine. Susie on the other hand...

Leah had to give her a sedative and tuck her into bed. She hoped in the morning, the woman would be back to her old self. Dan had volunteered to share the guest room and sleep on the floor in case she woke up and didn't know where she was.

It was all so surreal. She glanced at her husband. "Are you sure everyone who showed up in that truck is gone?"

"Either dead or missing. Dan and I counted four strangers dead. All of Greg's guys ran off. That's eight, nine if you count Greg."

Leah tallied the numbers in her head. "Assuming only four of Greg's goons were out there, that leaves two missing."

Grant nodded. "The man with the wound in his arm and one of his guys."

"Should I ask what you did with the bodies?"

"Better if you don't."

Leah nodded. "What about the truck?"

"It's as safe as it can be in Dan's garage and I've got the keys." Grant patted his pants pocket. "Assuming it's still there in the morning, we can load it up with all the gear and pick the best car to go with it."

"What about the motorcycle?"

Grant leaned back and blew out a puff of air. "We had to leave it at the car lot. A couple of teenagers are probably still trying to drive it home if they haven't wiped out in a ditch."

Leah stared at her husband. What more had the man been through that he hadn't explained? She sipped her hot chocolate. "I take it they weren't friendly?"

"Not exactly. But it worked out in the end."

Grant didn't elaborate and Leah didn't push. Whatever happened at the dealership didn't matter as long as Grant and Dan made it out of there without getting hurt.

She stifled a yawn and Grant poked her in the shoulder. "Go upstairs and lie down. You should at least try to sleep."

"I need to stay awake."

Grant smiled. "For the concussion, I know. But you can't fool me, Nurse Walton. I remember when you explained that the new guidelines are to let concussion patients sleep."

"But that's only if there's access to brain imaging software. We don't exactly have that here."

"No, but between me and you, we can assess the signs. Besides, there's only a few hours of night left. You'll be awake again before it's an issue." Grant leaned forward and kissed Leah on the cheek. "Get some sleep."

Leah eased the chair back with a frown. She didn't like leaving Grant all alone. As she stood up, a little white fluff ball trotted up and hopped up into the chair. Faith spun around and made herself comfortable in the seat Leah just left.

She smiled. That dog was something else. With one

last kiss from Grant, Leah dragged her weary body upstairs.

* * *

7:00 a.m.

Sunlight streamed through the open window as Leah gulped down another dose of Fish Mox. The stitched-up gash on her head barely swelled above her scalp and almost no redness remained. All traces of the infection were gone.

She wished she could say the same for the purpling bruise now spreading across the top of her cheek and up her eye socket. It hurt to touch any part of the left side of her face. The man Susie killed packed a massive punch.

Thank goodness he wasn't a problem anymore.

With one final look at her injuries, Leah left the bathroom. In an hour or so, they would be leaving her home behind, most likely for good. She looked at all the photos on the wall of the master bedroom. Grant on the beach in Florida, Leah covered in mud from a 3k race up north the year before. The pair of them on their wedding day.

Leah pulled down a handful of her favorite pictures, including one of her sister when she was only fourteen. She pulled the backs off the frames and slid the photos out. Just because she couldn't stay didn't mean she had to leave all the memories behind.

She pulled one of her favorite books off the shelf and tucked the photos inside. Faulkner could keep her family warm between his pages. After tucking the book into a duffle bag, Leah hurried down the stairs.

Everyone else was already awake and moving. Oliver shoved bits of electronic equipment into an oversized suitcase in the living room. Grant and Dan struggled with a tarp in the front yard.

Susie sat at the kitchen table with a mug of coffee in her hands. She nodded at Leah as she came down, but didn't say anything.

"Are you okay?"

She nodded.

"If you want to talk about last night—"

"I don't."

Leah almost winced. She couldn't imagine what Susie was going through, but she wished she could help. "Thank you. If it weren't for you—"

Susie held up a hand. "I don't want—"

"I get it. I'll leave you be." Leah turned and walked out the front door and into the morning air. A handful of neighbors stood on their porches, watching Leah's makeshift family work.

It might as well have been the start of a circus tent show.

She added her bag to the stack in the back of the pickup and rushed to help her husband. "Sorry it took me so long to get ready."

"You needed the sleep. How's your head?"

"Fine. My face took a beating, though."

Grant glanced up at her and winced. "Nice shiner."

"Thanks."

Leah grabbed one corner of the tarp and used a zip tie to secure it to a hook on the lip of the truck bed. "Will everything fit?"

"Between the truck and the Buick, we should be fine." Dan grunted as he secured another corner of the tarp.

"How's the arm?"

Dan glanced down at the bandage. "Fine. Hurts when I bump it, that's all."

"We should change the bandage tonight."

Dan nodded at Leah before getting back to work. Tension laced their little group and Leah shared in the unease. Leaving meant venturing off into the unknown, but staying was even worse.

After Greg's death, they could never trust anyone in the neighborhood. Someone would blame them. If it wasn't Jennifer and her sons, it could be Logan or any of the men who ran off the night before.

As Grant finished with the tarp, Will Greene, the neighborhood leader, walked up the road. He held up a hand. No one waved back.

"Looks like you all are leaving. Is that so?"

Grant rested a hand on the tarp. "I don't think we're welcome here anymore."

Will tried to smile. "We may have started off on the wrong foot, but that's no reason to run off."

Grant's jaw ticked and Leah wished they were on the same side of the truck. She spoke up. "Greg tried to break into our house. He had a group of thugs with him, ready to do us harm. If it weren't for those men who showed up, he'd have broken in."

Will rubbed at his chin as he focused on the sidewalk. "From what I've heard, you did a fine job of defending us."

Grant almost spit. "We weren't defending *you*. We were defending ourselves."

"Regardless, you saved us all a bunch of trouble."

Leah looked past Will to Greg's house. The shades were open and she could see two faces peering out at the street: David and Preston. Leah felt a pang of regret.

Greg's sons were without a father. And for what?

She cleared her throat. "What is it you want, Will?"

"I'm here to offer an olive branch of sorts."

"What for?"

"I was hoping you would reconsider leaving."

Leah shook her head. "Yesterday, you were willing to let Greg walk all over us. Take our things. Threaten us." She pointed at the burned-out shell of the truck she drove from Hampton. "He could have killed us all."

A tight smile creased Will's face. "With Greg gone, we need someone to defend us."

Dan snorted. "Then you better start going door-to-door because it sure as hell won't be us." He turned to Grant. "You ready?"

"Just about."

Grant turned and strode back inside. A few moments later, he reappeared with Oliver, Susie, and Faith in tow. He held up the keys. "Buick or Tacoma?"

Dan pointed. "Buick all the way. Those worn-out seats are like a hammock for my back."

Grant opened the door to the truck and Faith hopped in. Leah climbed in after. Within minutes, Susie and Oliver had claimed seats in the champagne-colored sedan and Dan had cranked the engine.

They were ready to go. Leah looked back at the house she expected to raise a family in and snuffed back unwanted tears. Grant reached for her hand. "It's the right thing."

She nodded, but didn't trust her voice enough to speak.

Grant cranked the engine and rolled down the window. He motioned at Will. "Good luck with your confiscation plan. You're gonna need it."

He tapped the hood and accelerated. Dan, Susie, and Oliver floated behind in the Buick, and together, the two vehicles left the neighborhood behind.

CHAPTER NINETEEN

GRANT

Foothills Motel
   Marietta, Georgia
   Tuesday, 4:00 p.m.

Smoke wafted past the hood of the Buick and Dan waved his hand in the air. He slowed and the left turn signal lit up on the bumper.

Grant glanced at the time. It had taken hours just to make it to Marietta thanks to thousands of stalled cars, looted storefronts, and the occasional run-in with desperate people. At almost ten days post-EMP and nine post-nuclear bomb, the Atlanta metro area was turning desperate.

Once they finished at the university, Grant vowed to stick to small roads and smaller towns and away from anything that could bring mobs. He was over that kind of trouble.

With their meager progress, it would take another full day at least to reach Kennesaw State, maybe two if the car kept overheating. He glanced at the gas gauge of the truck as he followed Dan into the parking lot of a budget motel.

Less than a quarter tank left. They would need gas before heading out as well. Dan parked the car in a secluded spot around the rear of the two-story building and Grant parked alongside him.

Everyone piled out onto the cracked pavement and Dan pointed at the car's engine. "It's shot. The temperature gauge hits the red within twenty minutes of driving. We push her any farther and we'll have to pile on top of the gear in the back of the truck."

Grant nodded. "The truck's almost out of gas. We passed a dealership a ways back. We can get everything stowed here and head back there to siphon some gas."

Leah stared at the truck with a grimace. "How about we find a storage rental place and just pull in? That way we don't have to unload."

"Last time I checked, storage places don't have showers." Oliver peered in the window of the restaurant attached to the motel. "Or a full bar."

Dan perked up. "Looked like I picked the right spot after all."

Grant motioned toward the row of rooms stretching off to the right. "Let's check them. Once we know it's clear, we can pick a few, unload, and relax."

Heading straight for the lobby, Grant wasted no time. He found a broken patch of concrete, picked it up and chucked it at the lower corner of the door. The glass shattered, falling in a sheet of pebbled pieces to the ground.

He stepped over the glass and behind the counter. A rack of keys, each labeled with a room number, hung on the far wall. Grant grabbed the entire thing and brought it back outside. "Everyone take eight. We can clear it faster if we split up."

"What if someone's here?" Leah picked out eight keys and held them in her hand. "Should we just shut the door?"

"Yell housekeeping and knock. Even after everything that's happened, people fall back on the predictable. If someone's inside, apologize and say you'll come back later."

"And if we run into trouble?"

Grant glanced around. The chances of that were slim. From everything he'd seen on the front and the back, the motel sat empty and alone. But he offered a suggestion. "Scream. No one will be very far away."

Everyone set off to clear their rooms. Grant's were located the farthest away on the front side of the motel. It was one of those two-story places with doors to the open-air hallways running the length of the building. With ten rooms on each side on each floor, they had forty rooms to clear.

He started with the room on the second floor closest to the end. "Housekeeping." Grant banged on the door and waited for a count of three before unlocking it. The room sat empty with a patterned bedspread from the eighties on the bed, threadbare carpet on the floor, and an even older bistro table and chairs.

No one lurked inside.

Grant closed and locked the door and moved on to the next, repeating the same knock and announce routine at each room until his eight were completed. He waved at Susie as she finished her last room upstairs. "Anything?"

She swallowed and spoke for the first time in hours. "No. I don't think some of these rooms have been opened in years."

He smiled. "You doing okay?"

She tucked her hair behind her ear and nodded. "I'm a little better. It'll take a while to shake it off, though."

They headed down the stairs together and found everyone else waiting by the lobby.

"Anyone see anything?"

Oliver spoke up. "One room had some luggage in it, but I think it was abandoned."

"Mine were empty." Leah handed her pile of keys to Grant.

Dan nodded. "Mine, too."

"I say we pick a few rooms down here on the first floor and unload the truck. Then we can poke around the restaurant and see if there's anything to eat."

"Who needs something to eat when there's whiskey?" Dan patted Grant on the back and headed toward the truck.

Two hours later, the sun cast a deep orange glow on the bar's windows and Grant eased into a booth. "The good news is there's an industrial-sized can of peach pie filling in the kitchen."

Dan glanced up from his half-empty glass of whiskey. "What's the bad news?"

"There's not much else." Grant raked a hand over his face. The last few days were beginning to take their toll. Lack of food. Lack of sleep. Shooting people in the street and dragging their bodies to his dead neighbor's house...

It all added up.

Dan shoved the bottle over. "Have a drink. It'll take your mind off it."

"No, thanks."

"You don't drink?"

"Not much. Makes me angry."

Dan nodded like he'd been there. "Used to be an angry drunk myself."

"What changed?"

"My wife died."

Grant blinked. He didn't know Dan ever had a wife. "When?"

Dan glanced up at the ceiling. "Ten years ago next month." He smiled at Grant with sadness in his eyes. "She was the best thing that ever happened to me, but the cancer was a real bitch. I started drinking when the tests after surgery showed the doctors failed to get it all."

He sipped some more liquor. "It did me in. I'd get mad, break stuff, scream at no one and everyone."

Grant knew the feeling. The few times he'd been drunk in his life he felt like Dr. Bruce Banner trapped in the body of the Hulk, just without the green skin or incredible muscles.

"When Kristy died..." Dan paused and cleared his throat. "There wasn't anyone to be angry for anymore."

"I'm sorry."

Dan waved Grant off. "It's been a long time."

"But you still miss her."

"Every damn day." Dan threw back the rest of the glass and set it on the table. "How 'bout those peaches?"

Grant stood up. "I'll get them. Maybe Leah's rustled up something else by now, too."

He found his wife in the kitchen, crouched in front of a metal shelf. "Anything good?"

She jumped and hit her funny bone on the counter. "Grant Walton, one of these days."

"We're going to find a wonderful place to settle down with a great big bed and I'm going to do terrible things to you all over it." Grant slipped his arm around Leah's waist and pulled her close. He couldn't imagine ever losing her. He kissed her lips before pulling back.

She smiled. "You okay?"

Grant nodded. "Just a little tired."

"I think we should sleep tonight and search for gas in the morning. You need the rest."

"I can keep going."

"Not forever." Leah reached for Grant and he let her pull him back into her arms. "Besides, I hear those motel room beds are pretty bouncy."

"Mrs. Walton, what has come over you?"

Someone behind them cleared a throat. Grant turned

around. Susie stood in the kitchen holding an armful of chips, crackers, and candy. "Sorry to interrupt."

Leah rushed up and relieved the other woman of her burden. "Where did you find all this?"

"The manager's office is also the storeroom for the vending machines. There's a ton of soda, too."

Grant exhaled. "Thank goodness. Now Dan will have something to add to the whiskey."

"Let the poor man have a night off. He needs the break. So do you."

Grant didn't have any interest in taking a break. He knew Leah meant well. Being married to a nurse meant he was constantly reminded about how best to take care of himself. But right now, all Grant wanted was a full gas tank so they could hit the road at morning's light.

If they wasted all morning searching for gas and set off in the afternoon, the Buick would overheat and they would have a repeat of today. He ran a hand through his hair. "We need to leave first thing in the morning so Dan's car won't overheat. I need to find gas tonight."

Susie set down the rest of the chips on the counter and smoothed back her hair. "I can come."

Grant tilted his head. "Are you sure?"

She nodded. "I know how to siphon gas." She smiled at Grant's shocked face. "I wasn't always this granola. If you look really closely you can still see the scar from my nose ring."

Leah giggled beside him. "Come on, hon. Let Susie come with you. Give Dan the night off."

Grant exhaled. "Okay." He turned to Susie. "Can

you find the gas cans? I'm going to grab a soda and we can head out."

Susie took off for the motel room with all the gear and Grant turned to his wife. "Be careful here. Dan's three sheets to the wind and Oliver's wrapped up in his computer. I don't like leaving you as the only one on watch."

Leah leaned forward and kissed Grant on the cheek. "I'll be okay. Besides, no one's here. As long as we stay quiet, I don't expect any visitors."

"We didn't expect a truck to come barreling into our neighborhood, either."

"I'll be okay. I promise."

Grant squeezed his wife's hand. "I'll be back as soon as I can."

"And then you're going to bed."

He grinned. "Yes, Nurse Walton."

CHAPTER TWENTY

GRANT

Marietta, Georgia
    Tuesday, 8:00 p.m.

Susie sat on her side of the Buick, not saying anything
while Grant drove to the car dealership. Unlike the lot
where Dan and Grant lifted the Cadillac, the Jeep,
Buick, Chrysler dealership sat full of shiny, oversized
paperweights that would never run again.

Grant pulled into the lot and killed the headlights as
he navigated to the largest concentration of trucks. "We
can hide back here. The pickups are tall enough to
conceal the car from the street."

Susie nodded. "They have the biggest gas tanks, too."

As Grant put the vehicle in park, Susie uncoiled a
loop of tubing they pulled off the dehumidifier in the
motel's office. She hopped out and headed over to the
closest truck.

While Grant grabbed two empty gas cans that Dan dug out of his garage, Susie fed the tube past the truck's fuel valve and down into the gas tank.

"So where'd you learn to siphon gas?"

Susie worked up a bunch of spit in her mouth and blew all the air from her lungs. She shrugged as she bent toward the tube. "Can you give me some light?"

Grant clicked on the flashlight and lit up the empty tube. Susie wrapped her lips around the clear plastic and sucked until a rush of gas flooded the tube. Then she pulled back and stuck the end of the tube in the gas tank and they both watched as the tank filled with gas.

"Gas tastes so nasty." Susie shuddered and spit a wad of phlegm on the ground. As the tank filled she answered Grant. "In a prior life, I was a juvenile delinquent."

Grant started. Susie the quiet gardener? He couldn't believe it. The tank Grant was holding reached capacity and he swapped it out for the second one. "Did you ever go to jail?"

"Juvie." Susie covered her throat with her hand. "Twice for possession. Never anything violent."

"Wow." Grant didn't know what to say. All this time, he'd pegged Susie as a straitlaced hippie who never saw the rougher side of life. "So when you shot that guy?"

She cut him a glance. "I was terrified. I might have been into drugs, but I never did anything like that. We were kids."

She shuddered and Grant wished he hadn't said anything.

"Every time I close my eyes, I see him punching Leah and then lunging for her with that look on his face."

Grant clenched his fist. "What look?"

"The I'm-going-to-kill-you kind." Susie rubbed at her shoulder. "I've got a nasty bruise from it, too. Whenever I forget what happened, then I move or bump it, and the memories come flooding back."

Grant reached out a hand and Susie flinched. He held it up in apology. "Sorry."

"It's okay." She shook out her hands and rolled her shoulders. "I've just got to get used to it, right?"

Grant wished he could say no, but the reality of the future they faced was grim and bleak. "Probably."

While Susie watched over the second tank, Grant hustled the first tank back to the Buick. He poured it all in and came back just as the second one filled. They swapped and he did it again, filling the car's fuel tank to capacity.

After switching to another truck and filling up again, they had two gas cans of fuel and a full tank of gas. Grant capped the second gas can and Susie pulled the tube from the tank.

"There's enough gas here to keep us going forever."

"A good long while, at least." Grant took both cans and hoisted them into the trunk. "Too bad we aren't staying."

Susie hesitated at the passenger-side door. "Do you really think we'll find out more at the college?"

Grant weighed the odds. "Yes and no. But it's somewhere to go that isn't here. And it's farther north."

"Why does that matter?"

Grant managed a small smile. "Canada's way bigger than the United States, has a tenth of the population, and hasn't lost power."

Susie stared. "You want to go to Canada?"

"It's an idea."

"Oliver said the same thing, but Leah didn't seem convinced. She said the border would be swarmed."

Grant's brow knitted. Leah and Susie already talked about where to go? He shouldn't have been surprised, but he was all the same. Leah hadn't wanted to leave home until she had no choice, but being a nurse, she always planned for the worst.

Usually he agreed with her, but not this time. He shrugged. "I think the border is enormous and Canada doesn't have enough military to police it."

"So you're advocating sneaking in? Becoming illegal immigrants?"

Grant winced. When Susie put it like that, it sounded terrible. He hauled himself up into the cab and waited until she climbed in as well before starting the engine. "I don't know. For now, let's focus on Kennesaw State. If we can connect with the outside world, we can figure out what to do and where to go."

Susie nodded and lapsed once more into silence. Grant didn't know what to make of her. She had the capacity to make tough choices, that much was true, but she didn't seem to want to. Maybe the safety and security of her adult life stole the part of her that put up a fight.

Grant backed the car out of the spot and headed back

toward the road. He clicked the headlights on and backtracked to the motel. As they neared, he slowed. A light bounced around a second-floor window. Grant turned off the headlights.

"What's wrong?" Susie sat up and squinted at the motel.

"See that light?" He pointed at the circular beam that rolled across an upstairs window and around a hotel room wall. "That can't be one of ours. We've already checked all the rooms."

"Maybe Oliver's looking for some equipment."

Grant shook his head. "No. That's someone else. I can feel it."

Susie shivered in her seat. "I don't think I can do this again."

Grant pinned her with a hard stare. "You don't have a choice." As he brought his eyes back to the motel, Grant rolled down his window. He stuck his head out, listening.

No noise.

Damn it. He eased the car forward and parked behind a closed Burger King next door. He grabbed the shotgun from where he'd stashed it under the seat and handed it to Susie. "Take this."

She stared at it in horror. "No."

He shoved it closer. "You have to. You might need it."

Her head shook back and forth like a bobblehead on a dash. "I can't. I can't do that again."

Grant pressed his lips together. Now wasn't the time for a freakout. "Susie. I need your help. Leah, Dan, and Oliver are in there. We need to go, now."

She sat in the passenger seat, frozen and unmoving.

Grant cursed and tried again. "Do you want someone to shoot you?"

Her eyes flicked up. "No."

"Then take the damn gun. Defend yourself."

Susie reached out and took the gun. It shook in her hands and she handed it back. "I can't. Just leave me here."

"Are you crazy?"

"Take the gun. Go save them." Susie's wide eyes stayed trained on the shotgun.

Grant took it back. "You can't stay here. If someone finds you, who knows what will happen."

Susie wrapped her arms around herself and looked out the window. "Go. Please."

Grant didn't know what to do. He couldn't leave her there, but he couldn't waste any more time. At last, he opened the door. "Come with me and hide. At least then I'll be able to hear if you get in trouble."

He hopped out of the Buick and held out his hand. After a moment, Susie slid across the bench seat and clambered down. Grant squeezed her hand. "Thank you."

Together, they took off for the motel and Grant hoped they weren't too late.

CHAPTER TWENTY-ONE

GRANT

Foothills Motel
    Marietta, Georgia
    Tuesday, 10:00 p.m.

Grant ran toward the rear of the motel, tugging Susie along behind him. He stopped at a set of stinking dumpsters filled with weeks' worth of garbage. "Stay here."

She shuddered and gripped her upper arms. "What happens if someone comes out?"

"Hide. Hopefully no one will look for you near the trash. It smells disgusting." Grant held out the shotgun one more time, but Susie shook her head.

He frowned and took it back. "I'll return as soon as I can."

"What if you don't?"

"Assume I'm dead."

Susie eased down to the ground, tucking herself between the dumpsters and the brick wall. With her jeans and long-sleeves, she blended into the dark. Grant sent up a silent prayer. If Susie stayed put, she might be all right even if Grant didn't fare so well.

He tucked his Shield into the holster and patted the extra magazine in his pocket before checking the shotgun. *Three shells.* It would have been better full, but three gave him something to work with. One shot with a 12-gauge and most people went down. Better to use the shotgun first and the handgun as backup.

The door to the rear of the kitchen loomed ahead, but Grant avoided it. He couldn't walk into a dark building with no idea who was in there or what was going on. However much he wanted to burst in guns blazing, he needed to be smart and patient.

Skirting the edge of the building, Grant kept below the windowsills and tight to the shadows, hoping to catch whoever was inside off guard. As he neared the motel office, voices materialized out of the hum of flying insects and chirps of cicadas.

"Once we find them, whatda we do with them?"

"Beat the shit out of 'em. Then find the keys to the truck."

Grant fumed. He wasn't even a day away from his house and already someone was trying to take what he had. How could they make it all the way to Kennesaw State? And once they did, how long could they stay?

Would every day be another battle? Would they

constantly have to keep eyes and ears open and expect the worst?

He crept closer. A brick held the door to the lobby open and the smell of smoke wafted outside. So far, he'd heard two distinct voices, but he couldn't count on that being all. Stucco adorned the lower half of the exterior lobby walls and Grant eased forward until he crouched beneath the first window.

With the shotgun ready, he risked raising up enough to see inside. A handful of men stood in a circle, dim shapes in the dark. One took a drag on a cigarette and turned to blow out the smoke.

Shit.

Even in the moonlight, he could make out the mane of dreads. The man Leah called Mr. Unicorn thanks to his ridiculous mask stood in the center of the group, pointing and giving orders. Grant spun around out of sight.

How had they found them? He thought back to the night before when Mr. Unicorn and the other man disappeared. They must have had a second car.

But Grant didn't until the morning. Did they wait for them all night in the neighborhood and follow them out of town? It was the only possibility.

Grant pinched the back of his neck. *What a fool I've been. If I'd been more careful, or if I'd done a better search, none of this would be happening.*

Turning back to the window, Grant squinted into the dark, struggling to see. Four other guys hunched together, but Grant couldn't make out much more than their size.

One scrawny guy kept shifting back and forth like he had to take a piss or was too cold to stand still. A big guy stood as still as a boulder, never once moving or tilting his head.

Slipping back down beneath the window, Grant thought it over. Could he take them all at once? Five men versus a shotgun and a 9mm. If they weren't armed, he had a chance.

He gripped the shotgun tight. *I could finish this right here.* Grant sucked in a breath, prepared to try, when the leader spoke again.

"Tito, hand 'em out man. Don't be stingy. Errebody gets a piece tonight."

Grant's bravado deflated.

Mr. Unicorn kept talking. "Hold up. Let me do it. You're always fumblin' around like a meth head without a fix."

Grant took a chance and raised back up. The men shuffled toward Mr. Unicorn one at a time as he handed out the weapons. "Dom gets the 12-gauge, Ace and Rocky get the Glocks, I get the 1911, and Tito you get the 20-gauge."

"Ah boss, why I gotta get the sissy gun?"

Without hesitation, he reached back and smacked Tito across the face. "How about no gun and I use you as target practice?"

Tito took the shotgun and eased back.

Grant dipped below the windowsill once more, a silent curse on his tongue. With that many guns, he couldn't take them on all at once. He'd have to isolate them and pick them off one by one. It would be slow and dangerous.

He had to have faith that Leah and the rest of them could hold on that long.

Faith. At the thought of the little dog's name, pain lanced Grant's heart. He hoped like hell she was safe in the gear room and not out there where she could be hurt. One swift boot to the side and she would be a goner.

Grant slipped back into the corner of the building where the darkness gave him cover. Moments later, the door to the lobby opened. Two men in hoodies walked out and headed toward the rooms.

He checked his watch. 10:30 *already.* Leah and the others had to be back in the rooms, sleeping off the last few days. He scrubbed his face. If the two goons heading that way found them first, it would be over before it began.

I can't let that happen.

Grant loped after the two men, adrenaline and fear coalescing in his heart. If Leah was asleep or not paying attention, she could be ambushed before she even had a chance to react. She would be dead before she even knew what hit her.

As the two walked down the open-air hallway, Grant followed in the shadows, keeping tight to the wall in hopes they wouldn't spot him. Clutching the shotgun in both hands, Grant thought about using it. He could rush them and fire before either man got a shot off, but the element of surprise would be gone.

Mr. Unicorn would hear the trouble. More men would come. Grant couldn't afford to put Leah and everyone else at risk. Not until he reduced the threat. These two would need to go quietly.

The men paused at the first door and fumbled with a set of keys.

"Yo man, gimme a light. I can't see nothin'."

A lighter flicked on and both men leaned over the door handle. At last, the door swung open. The one with the lighter held it up and eased into the room.

Grant seized the chance. He ran at them full tilt, rushing the door as the second man stepped inside.

Lifting the gun, Grant hit on instinct, slamming the butt into the back of the closest man's head. He crumpled to the floor.

The man with the lighter spun around. "What the—"

Grant didn't give him time to answer. He attacked instead, rage and fear turning him into an animal with a deadly weapon. He slammed the guy in the side of the head with the butt of the shotgun and the lighter flew across the room, plunging the space into darkness.

A fist landed hard in Grant's side and he staggered back. Pain radiated through his ribs. He struggled to breathe. A shape loomed at him and Grant reacted on instinct. The shotgun fit tight against his shoulder and the trigger pulled with ease.

The man who punched him grunted and staggered back, but didn't fall. Grant pumped the gun and fired again. His opponent sagged. Something clattered to the floor.

Grant reached into his pocket and found the flashlight. He pulled it out and clicked it on. A Glock 19 sat on the floor, a foot from the man bleeding out all over the threadbare carpet.

A shiver rocked Grant to the core. If he hadn't fired, he'd be dead. He picked up the Glock and dropped the magazine. Checking its round indicator, it appeared full with fifteen rounds. He eased the slide back slightly to confirm the round in the chamber, slid the magazine home, and then turned to the man he'd hit with the shotgun. Sprawled out and unconscious, he wasn't a problem now, but he might be later.

Grant aimed the Glock at the man's head and pulled the trigger. It fired smooth and steady. A well-used gun. He shoved it in his waistband next to the Shield and headed toward the door.

This time, there would be no loose ends.

CHAPTER TWENTY-TWO

LEAH

Foothills Motel
Marietta, Georgia
Tuesday, 10:30 p.m.

"You can't be serious. You've lived in Georgia your whole life but you're an..." Leah could barely utter the words. "Auburn fan?"

Dan raised his empty whiskey glass. "Go Tigers!"

Leah laughed and sipped her vodka tonic. The more she got to know Dan, the more she liked him. "Why didn't we hang out back in the neighborhood?"

"You were too busy canoodling with that husband of yours."

"I do *not* canoodle." Leah paused and glanced down at Faith where she slept on the mat beside her feet. "Okay, maybe I canoodle a *little*."

Dan raised his glass to his lips and frowned when it

came up empty. He reached for the bottle and tipped it over. A single drop landed on his tongue. "Damn. Guess they're out." He looked around. "Someone should fire the bartender."

Leah ran a hand down her face. While she'd been sipping, Dan had been full-on chugging whiskey. She didn't know how many he'd had, but more than enough to call it a night.

She rubbed her neck. Neither one of them should be drinking. Dan's blistered arm and her black eye and stitches didn't need alcohol slowing everything down. But she needed to relax. It had been a hell of a week.

Leah reached for the empty whiskey bottle. "Let's see if we can find some more." She grabbed the lantern they'd brought into the kitchen and headed out the door to the area behind the bar.

Dan struggled to follow. Leah reached for him and tugged, almost toppling over as they finally cleared the door. Faith darted through as the door swung on its hinges and sniffed around the glasses and bottles beneath the counter.

So far, they'd kept to the concealed parts of the motel, turning off the lights whenever they neared a window, but Leah couldn't read liquor bottles in the dark. She set the lantern on the floor and searched the stocked shelves. They wouldn't be visible for long.

As soon as she found another bottle, they could retire to the gear room and drink themselves into hangovers. As she squinted at the labels, a noise from the front of the restaurant sent Faith off on a barking tizzy.

Leah stood up, gripping the counter as a head rush made her dizzy.

"There you are!" Oliver rushed toward her, eyes huge and full of excitement. "You won't believe what I've found." He waved his computer in one hand and his glasses in the other and he talked so fast Leah couldn't understand a single word.

She held up the empty whiskey bottle. "Slow down. We can't understand you."

Oliver's eyes bounced back and forth as he took in Dan's beet-red face and the empty bottle. "You two got drunk?"

Leah stifled a giggle. "I'm tipsy. Dan's the one who's drunk. Slow down and tell me what you found."

Oliver puffed out a breath of air. "It's everything we wanted to know. I managed to get back online and—" His word cut off midsentence as the door to the restaurant opened and a boom echoed through the bar.

Leah stared in horror as blood sprayed from Oliver's chest. For a moment, he stayed standing, his lips contorting into an O as he looked down at his chest. But as the gunshot took its toll, Oliver crumpled to the floor.

The bottle slipped from Leah's fingers. As it hit the floor, a scream bubbled up her throat. She lunged for Dan. "Get down!" She dragged the drunk man beneath the bar.

Dan outweighed her by a hundred pounds or more. It took all her strength to haul him toward the floor. Another shot rang out. It shattered the mirror on the bar's wall and huge sheets of glass broke and fell all around them.

Leah sucked in a breath and reached for the lantern. She shut it off and plunged the area into darkness. How were they going to get out of there? She pressed her fingers to her temples and tried to think. *Damn vodka. If I live through this, so help me, I'm never drinking vodka again.*

Faith barked at her feet. She reached for the dog, and held the little fluff ball tight. Without a weapon, all they could do was hide. Leah leaned close to Dan and the stench of whiskey pushed her back. "We need to get out of here."

He nodded and tried to stand, but fell. "Go. I'll catch up."

"No! I'm not leaving you here."

The sound of boots near the bar shocked Leah into silence.

"I know you assholes are in here, so cut the crap and save me the trouble."

Leah swallowed. She recognized the voice from the night before. Mr. Unicorn himself. She looked down at Faith and then all around beneath the bar. It was too dark to make out much of anything. Opening the closest cabinet, Leah felt around and found an empty shelf beneath a stack of towels.

She shoved Faith into it before taking the little dog's face in her hands. "Stay." She whispered. "No matter what." Leah shut the door and leaned back. Her heart hammered in her chest and her clammy hands broke out into a full-on sweat.

Mr. Unicorn's voice grew louder. "Don't make me come find you."

At the end of the bar, the door led into the kitchen. If they could make it there, maybe they could get out of the situation alive. She turned to Dan. He still sat on the floor, butt surrounded by glass shards, rubbing his face.

"We need to go," Leah whispered. "This way." She tugged on his arm.

Dan lumbered up, half-falling twice before managing to stay somewhat vertical. If he made any more noise, they would be found out. Leah sent up a silent prayer and herded Dan toward the door, easing over bits of broken whiskey bottle as she worked her way toward the far side of the bar.

As she pushed the swinging door open, the wood above her head splintered. A bullet lodged in the trim board two feet above her head. Whoever had the gun wasn't messing around.

They had to get out of there and hide. Leah ducked through the open door, dragging Dan behind her. "Let's go!"

With one hand pulling Dan by the shirt sleeve and one held out in front of her, Leah scuttled into the dark. She bumped into a metal table and cursed at the pain.

The lantern still sat where she left it beneath the bar, useless now.

Feeling her way, Leah eased down the length of tables and toward the rear of the motel. Every place always had a back door through the kitchen. If they could find it and get outside, there were a million places to hide. She only hoped they could make it that far.

The door behind her slammed open on its hinges and a light spilled into the kitchen. Leah choked back a sob and ducked beneath the counter.

Mr. Unicorn held the lantern up high, sweeping it back and forth in one hand while he held a handgun in the other.

We're not going to make it. She turned back to Dan and whispered, "Please, we need to go faster."

"I can't." He shoved her hand off with a sloppy slap. "Go. I'll hold them off."

"No!"

"Do it." He heaved up and plastered on a smile. "I'll be okay."

Leah knew that was a lie. She stared at Dan as the lantern light hit her square in the face. It was too late. She scrabbled backward as Dan turned around.

Mr. Unicorn walked past the counter, staring straight at Leah. "First, you shoot me in the arm."

He pointed a handgun at her chest. "Then, you kill two of my guys." He stepped forward until no more than ten feet separated them. "Then, you steal my truck."

Dan moved to block Leah from view. He motioned for her to run. She shook her head. He wasn't going to die so she could get away. Not today.

Mr. Unicorn leveled his gaze on the pair of them. "How d'you think I feel today?"

Leah eased around Dan, despite his best efforts to

push her back. "Like you've got a hole in your arm and your feet are tired from all that walking." She glanced at Dan. "But he didn't do any of that." She thumped her chest. "I did."

"Leah!" Dan chastised her, but she ignored him.

Mr. Unicorn lifted his chin. "Is that right?"

"Damn straight."

He pointed the gun straight at her. "Then you deserve to be punished."

She swallowed. Visions of Grant finding her dead body filled her mind and bravado gave way to fear. She looked around for a weapon.

Mr. Unicorn laughed. "Not so brave now, huh?" He snorted. "Lucky for you I have a thing for pretty chicks with no hair." He turned toward Dan and fired.

The gun jerked and a round hit Dan in the gut. He grabbed at his stomach and blood coated his fingers.

"No!" Leah reached for him as he slid to the ground. She spun around, searching for something to stop the bleeding. A stack of kitchen towels caught her eye and she yanked them all toward her. Leah placed a wad of them on the wound and pressed Dan's hand on top before scowling at Mr. Unicorn. "You didn't have to shoot him."

"Didn't I?" He snorted. "What d'ya think this is, play time?"

Anger welled up in Leah and she stood up. "You could have taken your truck and left." She reached into her pocket and fished out the truck keys. She threw them at Mr. Unicorn's feet. "We aren't armed. We can't give you anything."

He looked her up and down and goosebumps rose across her arms. "Oh you can give me somethin', that's for sure." He bent and picked up the keys, ogling her as he rose back up.

She stepped back. "Never."

He grinned and two gold teeth came into view. "Good thing I like a challenge."

Leah bolted for the back, running as fast as her sneakers could manage. She reached the door when a burly guy with a tattoo covering his neck pushed it open. He had a gun of his own in his hand.

Leah backpedaled, but Mr. Unicorn blocked her in. She swung her head back and forth in a panic. *I can't die here. Not like this.*

She reached for a knife stuck in a butcher block on the counter. Long and sharp, it would do the job.

Mr. Unicorn laughed. "Put the knife down or I'll have Rocky shoot you where it hurts."

Leah swallowed and looked back at the other man. A bullet wound from a handgun might not kill her, but it could sure make her miserable. The knife blade wobbled in the air.

"I'm not going to ask again."

She set the knife on the counter.

Mr. Unicorn reached out and grabbed her by the wrist before forcing her arm behind her back. "Frisk her."

Rocky leered as he came closer, his hands roving up

her thighs. Leah screamed and pulled her leg back. He reached for her and with all her might, Leah shot her knee up. It hit his chin square underneath. His teeth smashed together, he fell back, and his head slammed into the wall.

Before Mr. Unicorn could do anything, Leah lunged for the knife with her one free arm, scrabbling for the handle as her captor yanked her back.

"Damn, girl, dontcha know when to quit?" He twisted her off-balance and pain shot up her arm and into her shoulder. The knife skittered away.

Leah sucked in a breath, ready to try again, when the butt of his gun came flying at her face. It came down hard and fast and before Leah could duck, it hit her temple.

Leah dropped to the floor, unconscious, again.

CHAPTER TWENTY-THREE

GRANT

Foothills Motel
  Marietta, Georgia
  Tuesday, 11:00 p.m.

With both men down, Grant grabbed the room key and pulled the door shut. He locked it and hurried toward the gear room when another gunshot stopped him still.

It came from the bar side of the motel.

Grant changed course. Shots meant action and danger and the real threat that something might happen to his wife. Blood whooshed through his veins to a frantic beat and Grant wiped his sweaty palms on his pants.

The motel lobby sat empty and Grant ran toward it, shotgun ready at his shoulder. It still had one shell left and he refused to waste it.

He eased through the lobby, past the front desk, and on toward the door to the restaurant and bar. With his left hand, he leaned forward to push the swinging door open. As his fingers touched the faded red paint, the door swung the opposite way.

Wood and glass smashed into his face and a sickening crunch sent a shooting pain through his nose and on up into his brain. His vision blurred and the tang of blood filled his mouth. Grant staggered back.

A man filled the space the door used to occupy. Grant swung the shotgun and fired the final shell. A shout tore from the man's throat and his shoulder jerked back, but he didn't go down. Most of the buckshot went wide.

The man yanked the shotgun toward him and dragged Grant off-balance. Pain made him slow and awkward. He stumbled and fell, barely getting a hand out to brace his fall.

His shoulder slammed into the ground and a boot plowed into the side of his head. Grant saw stars. The shotgun racked. His opponent didn't know it was empty.

Grant rolled across the floor as the man fired. Nothing happened. Grant reached behind his back for a gun. His fingers found the Glock first.

As he tried to pull it free, the man attacked, kicking him in the ribs. Grant curled up into a ball, sweat and blood loosening his grip on the gun. He faltered as the man kicked him again.

He could barely process, barely think. Visions of Leah dying in the other room swam before his eyes. *I can't save her if I die like this.* But he was only one kick away from unconsciousness and failure.

A frantic barking snapped Grant out of his daze. A ball of white fur jumped in the air as his attacker turned around. Faith's teeth sunk into the man's calf and Grant rolled onto his back.

With two hands wrapped around the Glock, he fired. The first shot went wide.

The man screamed and shook his leg, trying to rid himself of Faith. The little dog hung on.

Grant fired again. This time he didn't miss. The bullet pierced the man's left eye and the socket exploded. The man crumpled to the ground.

Grant fell back on the filthy tile as Faith climbed over his chest. He winced as she yipped in his face. "Thanks, girl." He gave her a pat with a blood-soaked hand and tried to sit up.

Three down, two to go. He rubbed at his eyes and blinked, trying to focus his mind and his vision. The blow to his head was brutal and he probably suffered a concussion. He leaned forward and searched the dead man for a gun.

He found a 20-gauge shotgun leaning against the wall. *What had the guy called it? A sissy gun?* Grant snorted and blood gushed out of his nose. *Bet he'd like to go back and use it now.*

As he reached for the shotgun, a scream snapped him to attention. Faith jumped up with a snarl. There was no mistaking that voice. It was Leah and she was in trouble. Grant hoisted himself up and wiped at the worst of the blood.

His nose was broken and a few ribs, too, but his legs

still worked. He could still shoot a gun. Grant grabbed the shotgun and edged past the dead man with Faith on his heels. He spit a wad of blood and phlegm on the floor as he crossed the restaurant.

As he moved into the bar area, the sight turned his stomach.

Oliver lay on the ground, a gaping wound in the center of his chest, face pale from lack of blood. It coagulated around his torso, soaking into the fifty-year-old carpet.

These men weren't after gear and weapons anymore. They wanted to hurt. Grant swallowed. The pain in his nose was no longer a distraction. It gave him focus, instead.

He eased toward the counter, checking for any sign of Leah or Dan. *Nothing.*

Faith urged him on, darting past him and behind the bar. She whined and Grant hurried up. Broken glass crunched beneath Grant's feet and he glanced down. A worn leather wallet sat on the floor. Grant picked it up and flicked it open.

Daniel Hostell.

Shit. Grant shoved Dan's wallet into his pocket and hurried to the end of the bar. He looked in through the circular window to the kitchen. His lantern sat on the kitchen counter, casting enough light to banish the gloom to the corners.

Faith pawed at the door and Grant pushed it open. She scampered around a stretch of metal tables and disappeared.

"Faith!" Grant eased into the room with the gun straight out in front.

The dog whined and Grant rushed forward. "Oh, no. Not you, too."

Dan sat against a tile wall, sweat coating his face and blood covering his hand. He clutched his belly and a wadded-up ball of towels. They dripped in blood.

Grant closed the distance between them and crouched at the man's feet. "Dan? Can you hear me?"

The older man roused, his head rolling to the side as he looked up. He tried to smile, but it ended in a grimace. "Hey, Grant. Good to see you."

"What the hell happened?"

"Those assholes from the neighborhood. Must have followed us here."

Grant swallowed. "Where's Leah?"

Dan tried to move, but fell back in a groan. "They took her."

"What?" Grant fought the urge to scream. "Where?"

"Out the back." Dan reached forward with his unsullied hand. "Go get the bastards."

Grant rose up, but froze in the hallway. "I can't leave you here."

"You have to. You can't let those men take Leah." Dan coughed out a laugh. "Don't worry. I'll be right here, waiting."

Faith seemed to understand his predicament. From the wound to Dan's stomach and the blood pooling around him, he probably wouldn't make it. How could he leave a friend to die all alone?

She padded over to Dan and turned around in a circle beside him before lying down. Grant nodded at her. "You stay with him, okay? When this is all over, I'll come back. I promise."

Grant handed Dan the 20-gauge and forced his emotions back. Leah still needed him. He couldn't stay and ease Dan's suffering. He had to hope that Faith could do the job and that she would still be there when he returned.

Because he would be back. No matter what.

With one final goodbye, he raced to the rear of the kitchen. Leah was out there and he would find her. Grant jerked open the door as a pair of headlights bounced through the parking lot.

Diving for cover, Grant rolled behind the dumpster as the truck came into view. The overhead light to the cab shone down on four occupants. Mr. Unicorn in the passenger window, trying to light a cigarette, another man behind the wheel, and...

Damn it.

Susie sat beside the driver, face stricken in fear, cradling the unconscious form of Grant's wife.

He jumped up and ran toward the Burger King where he stashed the Buick.

They can't get away. If he lost them, he might never find his wife. Gone was the pain in his nose or the side or his head or the throb of broken ribs.

He fell into the driver's seat and started the engine. As the headlights of the truck raced down the road, Grant eased out of the parking lot.

CHAPTER TWENTY-FOUR

LEAH

Location Unknown
Wednesday, 2:00 a.m.

The truck bounced over a curb and Leah jolted into consciousness. The first thing she saw was four pairs of shoes: a small set of women's hiking boots and a much larger pair of dirt-covered sneakers.

She blinked and sat up.

"Sleeping Beauty, welcome back."

Leah jerked at the voice.

Mr. Unicorn took a drag off a cigarette. "For a while, I thought I hit you too hard." He flicked the butt into the street and blew the smoke out the window. "Good thing I didn't. No one pays for a dead girl."

Leah shivered.

Next to her on the other side, Susie sat squished up against the driver, Rocky, the man with the spider tattoo.

Its legs inked up across his chin and body stretched down over his Adam's apple. Every time he swallowed, the spider's head moved.

They pulled up behind a building and Rocky put the truck in park.

Mr. Unicorn opened the door and hopped out. He motioned for Leah to join him. "I don't have all night. Come on."

She slid across the bench seat and hesitated at the door. Mr. Unicorn sighed. "If you don't come willingly, Rocky back there is going to pop your friend."

Leah twisted around. Susie sat motionless, the barrel of a handgun shoved tight against her temple. Leah pressed her lips together and stepped out of the truck.

Rocky shoved Susie out after Leah and she stumbled. Her hands flew out in front of her and she landed on all fours on the cracked and broken pavement.

Mr. Unicorn motioned toward the building. "Let's go."

Leah helped Susie up and slipped her arm around her. Together, they followed their abductor toward a rusted metal door. Rocky took up the rear, gun pointed straight at the two of them.

There was no way to run. Even if Leah left Susie behind, she'd be shot before she cleared the lot. The moonlight beat the shadows back and she would have to travel too far before reaching the safety of the dark.

As Mr. Unicorn held the door open, Leah cut a final glance outside. Her only hope was that Grant found them before it was too late.

Rocky pushed her and Susie through the door and Leah gasped. In her imagination, she'd conjured a pandora's box of horrors for the inside of the building: solitary chairs, zip ties, a dirty mattress on the floor.

What she saw couldn't be more different. From the outside, the building appeared abandoned. From the inside, it teemed with life.

Lights were strung up all across the ceiling beams. She traced the lines to a collection of solar panels pointing at the glass ceiling. *Smart.* The lights would stay off during the day and collect the sun, and at night, they powered the operation before her.

Stretched out in front of them were row upon row of supplies. Untold cases of water. Stacks of protein powder and powered supplement shakes. More Gatorade than she'd ever seen in her whole life.

Paper towels, toilet paper, batteries. The supplies went on and on and on. She swallowed. In the far corner, an arsenal flanked the wall. Guns of every size and shape from teeny tiny to massive lined a peg board. Beneath it sat stacks and stacks of ammunition boxes. Next to that, nestled fat clumps of cigarette cartons and bottles of liquor.

Leah turned to her abductor. Maybe the unicorn mask made sense after all. "How did you do all this?"

He puffed out his chest in pride. "I ain't no dumb sucker. The second the grid collapsed, we got to work."

"Where did you get everything? Stores?"

"To start." He hitched his thumbs into his belt loops. "But then we started hitting neighborhoods. That's where we got most of the guns. The pawn shops are locked up tight. It would take a grenade launcher to get in."

She snorted at the arsenal. "Don't you have one?"

"Workin' on it."

"Do you have some massive compound?"

His brow knit. "What d'ya mean?"

"Who's going to use all this stuff?"

Mr. Unicorn's face broke into a grin. "I am, to start. But once everything calms down, it's more of an insurance policy."

"Against what?"

"Everything." He ran his tongue across his lips. "He who has the most toys, wins." He motioned to Rocky. "Enough chit-chat. Tie these hoes up and get me a drink."

Susie's eyes went wide as she stared at Leah and her whole body trembled. Leah propped up a brave smile and reached for her. "It'll be okay."

Rocky laughed. "You heard the boss. Get moving." He pointed with his gun, herding Leah and Susie toward an unoccupied corner. As they walked, Leah ran through options in her mind.

She couldn't run or fight back. Not without a distraction first.

Once they were restrained, she might never get free. She ran a tongue across her teeth and turned around. "Before you tie us up or whatever," she flashed an apologetic smile, "I really need to pee."

Rocky ignored her. "Sit." He pointed at an area near

the corner. "One here." Susie headed straight for the spot and sat down with her back to the concrete block wall.

He moved and pointed to another spot at least ten feet away. "And one over here."

Leah did a little dance, crossing and uncrossing her legs. "I'm serious. I need to go. If I can't hold it, this whole place is going to reek like piss."

Rocky frowned. After a moment, he motioned for her to stay still. "Don't move or I'll shoot you." He shoved the gun in his waistband and walked over to the weapons.

Leah had her chance. She raced toward the supplies.

"Shit!" Rocky tore after her, pulling his gun from beneath his belt as Leah ducked behind a wall of Gatorade.

A shot rang out behind her. A case of Gatorade burst three feet from her head, spraying sticky liquid everywhere.

"What the—" Mr. Unicorn's shout filled the warehouse. "Don't shoot the loot!"

Leah ran down the aisle, ducking behind the stacks of bottles before sucking in a breath. There had to be a back door somewhere. *Yes!* She spotted a door with a push bar across it and took off, running as fast as she could.

As her fingers grazed the cold metal, an arm wrapped around her waist. Leah screamed and lashed out, kicking and bicycling her feet as the man lifted her off the ground. Her elbow collided with his gut and she gained an inch of breathing room.

It was enough. Her fingers slipped around the push

bar, and Leah hung on, tearing herself away from the man.

She stumbled into the door, shoving it open and sucking in a breath of freedom. But the man came right behind. A fist landed brutally hard into her left kidney and all the air whooshed from her lungs.

Leah fell to her knees. Pain radiated across her back and deep into her gut. All the possible injuries burst on her consciousness like fireworks. Kidney failure, blood in the urine, broken ribs.

The man came at her again and she swerved in time to catch a blow from his foot across her forearm. *Rocky.* He'd gone from shooting to brute-force Neanderthal and Leah didn't know how much more she could take.

Nausea rolled up her throat and everything burned. She staggered to her feet, saliva dripping from her lips and dribbling down her chin. This wasn't like the movies, where girls in tight leather hit and punched and saved the day. This was brutal. Horrific.

Rocky ran at her, spider tattoo bulging as he opened his arms to tackle her in a bear hug. Leah fell back on the ground and rolled, trying to escape his paws. He landed on her back, all two hundred or more pounds of him, and Leah couldn't even gasp.

He grabbed her arms and pinned them back before locking a zip tie around her wrists. He pulled so tight, the plastic dug into her skin. Blood slicked the teeth of the tie as he hauled her to her feet.

"You think you can get away from me?" His breath fanned hot and sour across her cheek.

Leah spat on the ground.

"You're lucky the boss wants you in good condition." He ground his pelvis against her backside and Leah fought down the panic. "Otherwise, you and me could have some fun."

With one hand wrapped around her upper arm, Rocky hauled her back inside. He dragged her through the warehouse and tossed her against the wall. She landed hard on her side and slid to the floor, legs going out from under her as she collapsed.

Rocky motioned to Susie. "Let that be a lesson. You try to escape, you end up like her. Or worse." He smoothed his hair off his face and straightened his shirt before walking over to the booze.

Mr. Unicorn sat in a leather club chair twenty feet away, watching the whole thing. He turned to Rocky. "Next time she tries to escape, all conditions are off."

Rocky grinned and called out to Leah. "You hear that, chica? Next time, you and me get to have some fun."

Leah leaned back against the wall and rolled her head to the side. She smacked her lips together to collect enough spit to speak. "How many are there?"

Susie glanced at Rocky with wide, terrified eyes. "Only those two."

Leah nodded. "Next time, I'll need your help." She adjusted her body to relieve some of the tension in her shoulders and inhaled through her mouth. She would need to conserve all her strength for whatever came next. If she didn't give it all she had, she probably wouldn't survive.

CHAPTER TWENTY-FIVE

GRANT

Unidentified Warehouse
  Marietta, Georgia
  Wednesday, 2:30 a.m.

Grant bit back a tortured scream. At least he knew Leah
was alive. He'd parked the Buick two blocks away from
the warehouse and crept up on foot in case the goons had
watchers stationed outside. But so far, he'd seen no one
except the leader and the guy who attacked his wife.

With Leah alive, but injured, he couldn't bust into
the warehouse without a plan. He needed to make sure
he could rescue Leah and Susie and make it back out of
there alive. For all he knew twenty guys could be in there,
fully armed and waiting for an attack.

Once again, he had to be patient. It didn't sit well
with him. Last time, he found one dead friend and one

with only hours left. If he took too long, he might find Leah the same way.

Grant checked both handguns. He had complete confidence in the Shield and two full magazines. The Glock hadn't failed him yet, but he'd rather work with the gun he knew. He shoved the Glock in his waistband and eased closer to the building, keeping the Shield low and ready.

His ribs ached with every breath and Grant had given up breathing through his broken nose half an hour before. Dried blood caked his cheeks and his head throbbed from the earlier kick. He was lucky to be alive, much less standing.

As he circled the building, he assessed the means of entry. One metal door near the parked pickup. One out back where Leah almost escaped. High windows too far up the wall to either see in or climb out of.

That left the roof.

A fire escape ladder was mounted to the wall about two feet above Grant's head. He holstered the Shield and gritted his teeth before jumping for the bottom rung. His ribs screamed as he stretched, but his fingers wrapped around the metal tube.

Hauling himself up an agonizing inch at a time, Grant clenched his jaw to keep from crying out. At last, he made it high enough to use his feet instead of his torso. He prayed for an easy way inside.

What he found was something all together different. Half of the roof was glass. Shaped like an upside-down V, the old-school atrium occupied the entire middle section of the rooftop.

Grant rubbed his cheek and flakes of blood fluttered to his feet. No one built businesses like it anymore. The warehouse had to be close to a hundred years old. Using the natural sunlight during day, it would have meant little to no electrical costs for the owner.

Now it meant Mr. Unicorn could see during the daytime as well as he could outside. Grant eased forward. The entire place was lit with strings of lights. Grant spied the solar panels lashed to the roof beams and shook his head.

He'd underestimated the mask-wearing gang. Not only did they figure out a way to have lights, but by the looks of the warehouse, they also knew how to hoard. Grant couldn't count the cases of water or the boxes of liquor. The place looked like a distribution hub for a shipping company, not an abandoned warehouse in the middle of nowhere.

Working his way around the windows, he searched for Leah. He found her slumped over in the corner with Susie a few feet away. She wasn't moving.

Grant clenched his fist and talked himself off the ledge. Maybe she was asleep or conserving her strength. Lack of motion didn't mean death. He tore his gaze from his wife and searched for the boss.

He found him in an overstuffed leather chair, one leg dangling over an arm, a glass of something in his hand. The man who fought Leah sat next to him, also drinking.

Two confirmed threats.

With systematic steps, Grant canvassed the rest of the warehouse from above. No one else was inside, but an entire back corner was stocked with weapons.

Grant leaned back as ideas percolated in his mind. They weren't expecting him, that much was clear. He could take his time and prepare the right kind of ambush.

After a few minutes, he decided on a plan and hurried down the fire escape.

It took ten agonizing minutes to fish out two unbroken beer bottles from the dumpsters behind the building next door, but Grant couldn't work his plan without them. After loping back to the Buick, he tore a few inches off the bottom of his T-shirt and ripped it into strips.

Into the beer bottles went gas from the red gas can Grant and Susie had filled up at the car dealership and then the strips of shirt. When they were ready, Grant rolled his shoulders and took a deep breath.

It was time to put his plan into motion. He opened the door to the Buick, pushed the cigarette lighter in and waited. As soon as it popped out, he gabbed it and ran, two bottles in one hand, lighter in the other.

He leapt for the fire escape ladder and ignored the pain. Every second mattered now. The moment he cleared the roof's ledge, Grant shoved the T-shirt from the first bottle into the end of the lighter and prayed.

If he'd taken too long, the coils wouldn't be hot enough to set the cotton on fire. After a few agonizing moments, smoke wafted up from the shirt and the fabric caught. Grant dropped the lighter on the ground and used the burning shirt to light the second.

With two burning Molotov cocktails in his hands, Grant hurried over to the glass roof. He set one bottle down and picked up a chunk of broken-off brick. With all his might, he threw it at the pane of glass directly over the relaxing men.

As the glass shattered, Grant threw the first bottle.

Screams and flames erupted in unison as the homemade bomb exploded on impact in a ball of flame. Grant lobbed the second bottle inside. Without even stopping to assess the damage, he took off at a run. He clambered over the side of the roof and almost fell down the ladder.

I have to get to Leah.

CHAPTER TWENTY-SIX

LEAH

Unidentified Warehouse
Location Unknown
Wednesday, 3:00 a.m.

Shattering glass roused Leah from an exhausted, pain-filled sleep. She jerked awake as the smell of burning gasoline assaulted her nose. What the—?

Fire leapt across the upholstered chair where Rocky sat. He jumped up, screaming and waving his arms as flames spread across his body. Leah watched in horror as he ran in circles, fueling the fire with the rush of oxygen.

Didn't he know the childhood adage: stop, drop, and roll? She'd had it ingrained in her head since before she could remember, and training as a nurse only reinforced it. Fires craved oxygen. Smothering the flames was the best way to put them out.

Rocky must have missed the memo. He ran straight

for her and Susie, the fire consuming his clothes and crisping his hair.

Susie screamed.

Leah rolled onto her side and struggled up onto her knees before forcing her legs to stand. With her arms still pinned behind her back, she couldn't do much more. She shouted at Susie. "Run!"

The other woman stared at Rocky as he fell to the ground. He would never survive.

Leah rushed toward Susie as Mr. Unicorn appeared in the heat of the flames. He almost growled in her direction and Leah staggered to a stop. "Susie! You have to run!"

Still, Susie didn't move. She just stood there, staring at Rocky's body as he turned from man to ash. Leah backed up. Mr. Unicorn circled the flames, easing around the worst of the smoke with an arm up to shield his face. He couldn't get through. The flames and smoke were too thick.

Leah glanced around, searching for something to cut the ties binding her hands. A massive shard of glass lay on the floor by her feet and she bent awkwardly to pick it up. It sliced her finger and she dropped it with a cry.

Mr. Unicorn tried again to reach her, circling around the flames closest to the wall, but they blocked his path, leaping across Rocky's body to a stack of cardboard boxes.

Leah spun in a circle, frantic for anything to help. A discarded sweatshirt was draped across a railing by the door and Leah ran for it, ignoring the shouts behind her. All she could focus on was getting free.

With the sweatshirt in her hand, she raced back to the glass and picked it up, now protected from the worst of its edges. Using it like a saw, she stuck it between her wrists and rubbed.

Pain shot across her skin. She couldn't tell if she was cutting her own skin or the ties, but either way, it was working.

Mr. Unicorn screamed at her. She kept sawing.

At last, the ties gave and her arms sprang free. Blood poured into her aching shoulders and dripped off her fingers. If she nicked an artery, she'd bleed out. She had to stop the bleeding. Using the glass, Leah hacked off the arms of the sweatshirt and tied them around her wrists to slow the blood loss, jerking her head up every few seconds to check on her abductor.

The flames still separated them. It hadn't taken more than a handful of minutes, but the fire now consumed most of the building. The two chairs were infernos, the massive stacks of toilet paper blazed, and the plastic around the cases of drinks began to melt.

She ran toward Susie. The woman still stood in the same place, almost catatonic. Leah reached for her as a section of flames broke between her and Mr. Unicorn. He rushed forward, gun in his hand.

Leah grabbed Susie and yanked her back. Together, they stumbled toward the door.

"You aren't getting out of here alive!"

Mr. Unicorn raised his gun. Leah dragged Susie faster toward the door. "Come on, we have to go!"

The door flew open and a figure appeared in the

doorway. Covered in blood and dirt with only half a shirt, Leah would recognize her husband anywhere. She shouted out a warning.

A gun went off. The bullet pierced Susie in the stomach, traveled straight through her body, and into Leah's side. It grazed her ribs and kept going, lodging in the concrete behind her.

Susie sagged in her arms. "No!" She yanked on the other woman as Grant rushed into the room.

Her husband screamed. "Get down!"

Leah ducked as Grant opened fire. Mr. Unicorn ducked and ran, reaching safety behind flaming paper towels before Grant could kill him.

No! He couldn't get away.

Leah refused to be a victim the rest of her life, always watching over her shoulder, waiting for a man in a unicorn mask to hunt her down. She eased Susie to the floor and shouted at her husband. "Go! Don't let him get away!"

It was all the encouragement Grant needed. He turned and ran back out the way he came in.

Leah sucked in a breath, but inhaled mostly smoke. She gagged as she hunched over Susie's body. The wound was vicious, tearing through her entire midsection at an angle and causing untold damage to her intestines and other vital organs. Leah reached for the woman's neck to confirm what she already knew.

Susie was gone.

Leah cursed and ran a hand over the stubble across her scalp. All of their new friends. Every single person who stood up for her and Grant in the neighborhood. *Dead*. And for what? Leah sobbed out a breath and looked down at her own wound. Blood soaked her shirt and she lifted up the fabric with a wince.

Burned skin edged a six-inch gash from her belly button to her side, but the bullet didn't penetrate. She was lucky, unlike Susie.

Leah looked up at the flames torching the rest of the building. She had to get out of there. With a grunt of effort, she stood. So many supplies. So much food and water and ammunition, wasted.

The thought of leaving everything behind turned her stomach. There had to be a way to save something. She skirted the worst of the flames, holding the tied-off strips of sweatshirt up to her face.

The chairs where the men were sitting were almost burned out, the flames no more than a foot or two tall. Leah edged their heat, easing past the piles of ash and soot and reached the armory.

She grabbed a duffel bag from the far wall and filled it with everything she could reach: handguns and shotguns and cases and cases of rounds. She didn't know if they matched up, but she didn't have time to figure it out.

Soon, even the guns would burn. She hoisted the heavy bag onto her shoulder and headed toward the rear door, stopping only once more for a bottle of liquor. With her hands full, she rushed outside.

CHAPTER TWENTY-SEVEN

GRANT

Unidentified Warehouse
   Marietta, Georgia
   Wednesday, 3:30 a.m.

Grant tore after the only threat left. Mr. Unicorn wouldn't get away. With his gun in one hand, Grant ran around the building, avoiding the heat of the flames that were now so tall, some even escaped through the broken glass roof.

As he cleared the last corner of the building, a shot rang out. Grant skidded to a stop. As he dove for cover, three more shots followed.

Grant didn't know what kind of a weapon Mr. Unicorn had or how many rounds, but he couldn't hide and let him get away. They would never have peace with him out there.

Leading with his gun, Grant shot toward the direction of the incoming bullets. With two guns, he could waste some ammunition. He pulled the trigger over and over as he rushed forward. The Shield ran out of ammo and he shoved it in his holster before yanking the Glock from his waistband.

Thanks to the flames, Grant could see the truck sitting alone in the parking lot. No sign of Mr. Unicorn anywhere near it.

Damn it.

Grant rushed for the truck, gun up and ready. Movement caught his eye. *There!* The man he was after crouched behind the rear wheel, his knees poking out beneath the truck bed. Grant dropped to a crouch and fired.

The bullet went wide.

Mr. Unicorn ducked back, hidden by the truck.

Grant closed the distance, keeping low and aiming for the space the man had been. Another series of shots rang out. Three, four, five.

A searing pain caught Grant in the shoulder and he jerked backward. He stumbled to the ground five feet from the truck door. With one palm on the ground, he forced himself back up.

Mr. Unicorn yanked open the driver's-side door to the truck. Grant struggled forward. He reached the passenger side as the truck's engine revved to life. As he grabbed the door handle, the truck lurched forward.

Grant swung by his arm, slamming into the fender before swooping back around and crashing into the door.

His feet hit the running board and he scrambled on while Mr. Unicorn punched the gas.

Using his wounded arm, Grant forced his body up enough to clear the open window. Mr. Unicorn sat in the driver's seat, pressing the gas pedal to the floor. Grant brought his gun into position.

Mr. Unicorn jerked the wheel to the side.

Grant lost the shot.

As the truck took a corner way too fast, Mr. Unicorn brought up his gun. He fired. It clicked. He fired again. Nothing.

Grant almost laughed in relief. He aimed again and opened it up, pressing the trigger over and over. Mr. Unicorn didn't stand a chance.

The truck slowed and Grant clambered into the seat. He yanked the driver's-side door open and shoved Mr. Unicorn out before taking over behind the wheel.

Grant turned the truck around and headed back to the warehouse, leaving the man's corpse to bleed all over the middle of the street. He bounced over the curb and came to a stop ten feet away from the rear entrance.

Leah stood outside, a bag over her shoulder and a bottle of alcohol in her hand. She smiled and Grant waved her over.

"Is it done?"

"It's done. They're all dead."

She nodded and climbed up into the cab. After fastening her seat belt, Leah unscrewed the bottle and took a long drink. She handed it over.

Grant stared at it for a moment. "Since when do you drink gin?"

Leah let out an exhausted laugh. "Let's just say I've come to see an old woman's point."

The liquor burned the back of Grant's throat and he handed it back with a grimace.

His wife capped the bottle and leaned back in the seat. "Take us back to the motel."

CHAPTER TWENTY-EIGHT

LEAH

Foothills Motel
  Marietta, Georgia
  Wednesday, 4:00 a.m.

Leah eased out of the truck and tugged the massive duffel bag behind her. She was bruised, bleeding, concussed, and more. Every step felt like a marathon.

Grant hustled up to her, his 9mm in his hand. Leah sagged beneath the weight of the duffel and their ordeal.

"Do you think Dan—" One look at her husband's blood-caked face and she didn't need to finish.

Together, they eased through the lobby, stepping over the dead body of a man who tried to kill them before finding Oliver where he died in the middle of the restaurant floor. Leah swallowed hard and kept walking.

The bar area was destroyed. Glass littered the floor and covered the wood countertop. Grant's flashlight reflected off the shards as Leah bent to open the cabinet where she'd stuffed Faith.

It was empty.

"No!" She stood up in a rush and a wave of nausea forced her to lean against the counter.

"What is it?" Grant reached for her.

How could she tell him? Her husband loved that dog. She licked her cracked lips. "I put Faith in there before those monsters—" She choked on the implication and Grant took her hand.

"It's okay. I know where she is." He eased past her and pushed the door to the kitchen open.

Leah followed. The lantern still sat on the countertop and beneath it, Dan's lifeless body sprawled out on the floor. Even from a few feet away, Leah knew he was gone. His skin was ashen, his arms hung limp, and his whole body sagged in release.

Tears pricked her eyes. Dead. Another friend, dead.

Grant knelt beside Dan and reached for the wad of towels in the man's lap. They growled.

"Shhh. Faith, it's me."

The bundle of towels rose up and shook and out came a little blood-stained dog.

"Faith!" Leah fell to her knees in relief. Tears pricked hot and heavy in the back of her eyes and she let them fall. "You're alive!"

Grant ran a hand through her fur and she climbed over Dan's cold leg to rub her head against his chest. He pressed a hand against his lips.

Leah reached for her husband and he wrapped her

up in his arms with Faith between them. Together, they sobbed.

Tears streamed down her face and Leah let go of the adrenaline, fear, and rage that kept her going the past week and a half. Everything that happened, everything she endured, it all changed her.

Gone was the woman who blindly trusted other people and rushed in to help no matter what. In her place was someone else. Leah didn't know who she was now or what kind of person she would be a year down the road, but one thing held true: she was a survivor.

No matter what life threw at her, from bombs to angry neighbors, to people hell-bent on taking what she had, she would make it out alive. She squeezed her husband's hand. So would Grant.

She leaned back and wiped her face. "Let's get to the gear." She looked down at the wound on her side with a grimace. "We need to clean and treat our injuries."

Grant exhaled. "I'll bury Dan and Oliver in the morning."

Leah forced her exhausted body to stand and she tried to pick up the bag full of guns. She couldn't lift it.

Grant reached over to help. He grunted as he lifted the strap onto his shoulder. "What's in this thing?" He unzipped the top and pulled the side apart before looking at his wife with wide eyes. "Leah Walton, you are the best wife a man could ever have."

She smiled and tugged him toward the motel rooms. "Don't say that yet. I haven't fixed your nose."

Half an hour later, Leah stood under the cold water

of a motel shower. The water pressure left something to be desired, but as long as the water still ran, she was thankful. Blood and sweat and grime slipped from her body like a snake's skin and she emerged from the shower reborn.

Standing in front of the mirror, she held a lantern up in the air. Hacked-off hair. Stitches. Black eye. Bruise spreading across her cheek and down her neck.

And that was just her head.

Then came cuts and scrapes up and down her arms. The gashes on her wrists. The bullet graze across her middle.

So many injuries. She frowned. They weren't injuries; they were battle scars. She was a warrior in this new, changed American landscape and she would persevere.

Leah eased on underwear and a bra before walking into the room. Her husband sat on the edge of the bed, clean, but beat like a piece of tough steak. She stared at his injuries.

Bullet wound to the shoulder. Broken nose. Bruising across his stomach that probably meant broken ribs. Scrapes all over.

She sat down beside him and laughed.

"What's so funny?"

"We look like a couple of cast-offs from *Fight Club*."

Grant chuckled. "No, we still have all our teeth. Hand me that bottle of gin."

She handed it over and her husband took a huge swig. "All right. Set my nose before I change my mind."

Leah nodded and stood up. "This is going to hurt."

Her husband raised one eyebrow and she bit back a grin.

"Just warning you. Try not to move, okay?" Leah stood directly in front of him and assessed the damage. Her husband's nose canted to the right a third of the way down the bridge. If she didn't fix it, he'd never breathe right again.

Leah climbed on the bed behind him and planted her knees firmly against his back. She brought her hands around his front and steepled her fingers together above his nose.

"Ready?"

"As I'll ever be."

Leah sucked in a breath, pressed her hands together as hard as she could and slid them down Grant's nose. The cartilage and bones crunched and gritted as they realigned.

Grant gripped the bed cover, almost ripping it in two, but he didn't move his head. As Leah pulled away, he exhaled and sagged forward.

She clambered off the bed and came around the front. "Let me see."

Grant blinked a few times, opening his mouth and closing it as he sat up. "I think that hurt worse than getting shot."

Leah squinted at his nose. Better. Not perfect, but better. "How's the breathing?"

Grant snuffed. "Improved."

"Good. Now don't bump it or move it for a couple weeks."

Grant leaned back on the bed. "With our track record, I'm not sure that's possible."

Leah opened up the trauma bag they'd brought with them from the house and set to work on herself, cleaning and treating the damaged skin from the gunshot before bandaging her wrists. There was nothing she could do for the bruises on her face or the concussion she most likely suffered.

She twisted around to look at her lower back. "Do I have bruising down here?"

Her husband peeled himself off the bed and brought the lantern over to look. "It's just beginning. Looks like a fist."

Leah exhaled. "Right to the kidney. I have to keep an eye on the symptoms."

After she finished treating herself, she dressed and turned back to Grant. His wounds were mostly superficial, apart from the gunshot. The bullet went straight through the muscle of his shoulder.

It would heal as long as they kept it clean.

She fished out the Fish Mox and handed him a pill before taking one herself.

"Is that it?"

Leah climbed up on the bed and slipped beneath the covers. "It's the best I can do."

Faith slept in the middle of the bed, exhausted and filthy. They would need to bathe her in the morning, but for now, the little dog needed to sleep. So did Leah.

She snuggled against the pillow. "Do you think we're safe here tonight?"

Grant slipped under the covers on the other side of the bed. "The door is locked, a chair is shoved beneath it, and there are dead bodies all over out there." He fluffed the pillow and clicked off the lantern. "If anyone manages to find us here in the next few hours, then so be it. We have to sleep."

He reached out across the bed and took Leah's hand. "I love you."

She mumbled as sleep took hold. "I love you, too."

* * *

Thursday, 2:00 p.m.

Leah woke to bright light filtering into the room. She reached out for Grant, but his side of the bed was cold. With a groan, she eased her sore, overworked body into a sitting position and checked the time.

Whoa. She'd slept the entire morning away. As she wiped the sleep from her eyes, Faith trotted up, as clean and fluffy as Leah had ever seen her. She smiled. "Guess my husband's been busy."

She reached down and rubbed Faith beneath the chin. "Let's go find him and find you something to eat."

The little dog yipped and turned in a circle. Leah stood up, slipped on her shoes, and grabbed the handgun sitting on the table. First order of business, her husband was going to teach her how not just to shoot, but to be a good shot.

From now on, she would always be ready to defend herself and she would never take her safety for granted. Leah exhaled and opened the motel room door.

The bright afternoon sun warmed her face and she stepped out into the light.

CHAPTER TWENTY-NINE

GRANT

Foothills Motel
    Marietta, Georgia
    Thursday, 2:00 p.m.

Grant shoved the last heap of dirt on top of Oliver's grave and leaned against the shovel. His ribs ached and his shoulder needled him every time he moved, but he couldn't leave their bodies to rot in the motel.

It had been a hell of a couple of weeks. From the moment he overheard the pair of hackers discussing the threat to now, it had been nonstop fear and focus. Until last night, he wasn't sure how much sleep he'd had. A few hours, maybe.

At least for the moment, he knew his wife was safe and they could catch their breath.

Across the parking lot, the door to the gear room opened and Leah stepped out into the sunshine. The light glinted off the fuzz of hair growing back on her head and Grant stopped to marvel.

He'd always admired his wife's quiet strength and ability to face death and loss every day as a nurse. But he'd never thought of her as a fighter until now. Watching her defend herself, seeing her fight to the last inch of her strength and capacity...

It did something to him. She was more than just the woman he loved. She was his partner. His forever.

Grant smiled as she closed the distance between them. Faith scampered beside her, clean and happy in the sunlight. "How are my two ladies this fine afternoon?"

"Sore. But we'll recover." Leah motioned to the shovel. "I could have helped."

Grant shrugged. "I couldn't sleep. It needed to be done."

Leah rubbed her bare arms. "What about all their things?"

"I buried their identification with them. Seemed right somehow." Grant rubbed his face, careful to avoid his nose. "I don't know what good Oliver's computer will do, but I found it in the bar."

Leah started. "When he was shot, he was all excited. He'd rushed in talking about getting online and finding something." She shook her head. "I'd forgotten all about it after everything that happened."

"Did he say any more?"

"No." She swallowed. "He died before he could."

Grant picked up the shovel. "Let's get on that

computer and see if we can figure out what he found." He strode toward the scene of the fight, stepping over the dried pool of blood where he'd killed the man the night before.

The three men he killed at the motel were in the dumpster out back, rotting along with the rest of the garbage that would never be picked up. They didn't deserve a proper burial.

Grant bent down to pick up Oliver's computer while Leah brushed past him to head toward the kitchen. "I'm going to fix Faith something to eat. I think I saw cans of chili back here yesterday."

While his wife disappeared into the kitchen, Grant took Oliver's computer to a booth in the sun and opened it up. The screen turned on and a chat window appeared.

It was a conversation between Oliver and MFly, the handle Grant hoped was Midge.

Grant leaned in to read.

Ollie91: Charlotte Hack-A-Thon. WelSoft guy, short hair. Gave you a hard time. Says he knows you.

MFly: He alive?

Ollie91: Made it to Atlanta. It's bad here. Bomb destroyed everything for miles. No power.

MFly: Bad in Chicago, too. Business district gone.

Ollie91: How are you online?

MFly: Escaped. Everywhere is dangerous.
More to this than what you think.

Ollie91: Where are you?

MFly: Powers that be aren't what they seem.
Safer to leave.

Grant paused. Powers that be? He ran a hand over
his head. Who could she mean? The government? Had
someone mobilized in the Midwest? Were they trying to
institute order up there?

He scrolled the chat.

Ollie91: Why?

MFly: Can't say more. Eyes everywhere.

Ollie91: Where should we go?

MFly: Away.

Ollie91: Where? The plains? Somewhere
rural?

MFly: Think bigger. Colder.

Ollie91: Canada?

There wasn't an immediate response. Oliver pinged
the hacker girl a few more times before she answered.

MFly: Where the loon meets the green, you'll

find the meadow. It's secure. Come if you're
able. You need to get out while you still can.

Oliver pressed the girl for more information, but she
wouldn't deliver. Grant leaned back with a frown. She
was giving him directions, but to where? He minimized
the chat window and a map filled the screen.

Canada.

Smack in the middle were a collection of towns. Loon
Lake to the west, Green Lake to the east, and smack in
the middle, Meadow Lake. He leaned back. Meadow
Lake, Saskatchewan.

Oliver found out where she was and the girl claimed it
was secure. Grant looked out the window. It had to be over
two thousand miles away. Could they make it all the way
to Canada? Could they leave the United States behind?

The door to the kitchen swung open and Leah
emerged. She stopped when she saw his face. "What
is it?"

"Oliver found one of the hackers at the convention."

"You mean the kids who warned you about
the bombs?"

He nodded. "She's in Canada."

Leah walked toward the table and slid onto the bench
seat across from Grant. "Why?"

"She says there's more going on than we realize. That
nowhere in the United States is safe." He leaned back.
"She told him to leave."

"And go where? Did she tell him where she is?"

"Not exactly, but Oliver found it." Grant turned the computer around to show Leah the map. "Meadow Lake."

"Saskatchewan?" Leah's eyes went wide. "Isn't that mostly trees and snow?"

"And a small town, population just over five thousand."

Leah exhaled. "Do you want to go?"

"It's two thousand miles."

"Can we make it that far?"

"It won't be easy." Leah looked down at Faith, who'd hopped up onto the bench beside her. "Do you trust her?"

"The girl?" Grant thought it over. She hadn't lied to him. Even when she was terrified and didn't know who he was or what he was about, she'd told him the truth. "I have no reason to doubt her. If it weren't for her, I'd be dead."

Leah nodded, but didn't say any more.

Together, they both looked out the window at the parking lot and the broken city beyond. Ever since the bombs detonated, they had been living in a waking nightmare.

Grant had almost died more times than he could count; Leah, too. If they stayed in the United States, would things get better? Would they live to see it?

The thought of leaving pained Grant. He wasn't a deserter or an asylum seeker or any of those things. But if things were happening that he didn't understand, then leaving might be the best choice.

Grant reached for his wife's hand and smiled. "How do you feel about a road trip?"

* * *

Thank you for reading *Survive the Panic*.

Want to know how it all started? Subscribe to Harley's newsletter and receive *First Strike*, the prequel to the *Nuclear Survival* saga, absolutely free.

www.harleytate.com/subscribe

If you found out the world was about to end, what would you do?

Four ordinary people—a computer specialist, a hacker, a reporter, and a private investigator—are about to find out. Each one has a role to play in the hours leading up to the worst attack in United States history.

Will they rise to the occasion or will the threat of armageddon stop them in their tracks?

ACKNOWLEDGMENTS

Yes! I'm so excited to launch book three in my Nuclear Survival saga. I've had in my mind since the beginning of this series where I've wanted these characters to go and I'm happy to see them on their way.

Book four in the Nuclear Survival saga will jump time and location - back to the beginning of the attacks and up north to Chicago. Midge, the hacker girl who clued Grant in to the impending attacks needs to save her mom, and maybe help save the rest of America, too. Her story will be the *Northern Exposure* series and I hope to launch it this fall.

As I've mentioned before, if you're familiar with the locations I write about but are confused when you don't see street names or places you know, that is intentional. Although I try to be as realistic as possible, I do take liberties with regard to names, places, and events for the sake of the story (and to not ruffle real life feathers!). I hope you don't object and can still go along for the ride.

If you enjoyed this book and have a moment, please consider leaving a review on Amazon. Every one helps new readers discover my work and helps me keep writing the stories you want to read.

I'll be back soon with a welcome revisit to old friends in book eight of *After the EMP*, launching late this summer.

Until then,

Harley

ABOUT HARLEY TATE

When the world as we know it falls apart, how far will you go to survive?

Harley Tate writes edge-of-your-seat post-apocalyptic fiction exploring what happens when ordinary people are faced with impossible choices.

The apocalypse is only the beginning.

Contact Harley directly at:
www.harleytate.com
harley@harleytate.com